EMERALD EARTH

—·—

BOOK ONE OF THE WITCH BROTHERS SAGA

ADAM J. RIDLEY

BLAKE ALLWOOD PUBLISHING

Adam J. Ridley
Visit my website at adamjridley.com

Printed in the United States of America
Box Elder, SD
First Printing: June 2022
Blake Allwood Publishing

Ebook ISBN: 978-1-956727-28-9
Paperback ISBN: 978-1-956727-29-6
Library of Congress Control Number: 2022911643

Content Warnings

Homophobia
Controlling Parents
Explicit Sex Scenes
Child Abuse
Violence

Join Blake's email list to get advance notice of new books and receive his occasional newsletter:

www.blakeallwood.com

<table>
<tr><td>

MM Romance
By Blake Allwood

Transitions Series
Aiden Inspired
Suzie Empowered (MF Romance)
Bobby Transformed

Chance Series
Love By Chance
Another Chance <u>With</u> Love
Taking A Chance <u>For</u> Love

Romantic Series
Romantic Renovations (1)
Romantic Rescue (2)
Romantic Recon (3)

Melody Series
Melody of the Heart
Melody of the Snow

Road to Rocktoberfest Anthology
Changing His Tune - 2022

Coming Home Series (2023)
A Long Way Home
Family Home
Down Home
…and many more

Novellas
Tenacious
Moon's Place

</td><td>

Romantic Fantasy
By Adam J. Ridley

Big Bend Series
Love's Legacy (1)
Love's Heirloom (2)
Love's Bequest (3)

The Witch Brothers Series
Emerald Earth
Diamond Air
Ruby Fire
Sapphire Water

</td></tr>
</table>

ACKNOWLEDGMENTS

Special thanks to the following amazing people who helped me get this book finished and into your hands.

Jo Bird: Editor
Alma Alexander: Editor
Renee Mizar: Editor
Ann Attwood: Proofreader
J.P. Jackson: Beta Reader

And of course, a big thank you to my husband who puts up with my endless stories and handles the formatting and final publishing of all my books.

CHAPTER ONE

PROLOGUE – TWENTY-FIVE YEARS BEFORE:

CREA

"NO SON OF MINE is going to be with another man!" my father yelled, his face flushed with anger.

My older brother, Lance, gave back as good as he was getting, "What are you going to do, kill every guy I date?"

My father looked at him, and I knew that was exactly what he thought.

"Dad," I said, trying to soothe the situation, "I'm gay too. I don't know why you're so upset. Grandma said it's normal for our family. Your grandpa and great-grandad were both bi."

Dad turned toward me, his eyes like targeted missiles. "Crea," he said, then pointed his finger at me. "You and he are both abominations."

"Oh, please," Lance replied. "Like you're going to throw the Bible at us? You're from a long line of pagans, Dad. Why are you pretending you aren't?"

"The devil is in each of you," he said, and stomped out of the room. Lance rolled his eyes. Dad had been a devout witch, until Mom had convinced him to run for political office. Now he was acting like some kind of evangelical minister.

Lance rolled his eyes again when Mom came in behind our father's dramatic exit, saying, "You know your father has found the Lord, and you need to as well! I should never have let you boys be around that witch." Crocodile tears poured down her face as she spoke.

"I want you out of my house," Dad said, storming back into the room. "Both of you, out!"

Our younger brother Kyle came into the kitchen then, sobbing. "You might as well kick me out too, Dad. I'm... um gay, or... bi too." Poor Kyle had approached us before this started, telling us he thought he might be gay, but that he wasn't sure. Unfortunately, we'd assured him it wouldn't be a problem. How wrong we'd been.

Kyle's confession was more than our dad could handle. He might have chosen a new religion, anything he could do to promote his new political ambitions, but he still had his powers.

Dad's face began to glow as he screamed at us, *"No progeny of mine will taint the family name with sinful faggot love. Ever!"* He pointed at the three of us standing together. *"You will never know the love of another man. I forbid it, I forbid love for you three! Now get out!"*

A breeze stirred through the room. I felt cold and hot, a thousand pinpricks torturing me all at once. Dad and Mom both wore shocked looks as the energy in the room swirled around us. Realizing what he'd done, he paled.

"You see that? You can't deny who you are. You want to play that way, fine... fuck you," Lance challenged our father. His eyes changed from brown to light blue, the way Grandma's did when she was about to cast a heavy spell, then raising his hands, he looked toward Dad. *"Vengeful hate you dare to cast, toward your children no love shall last, once in your arms you held us three, now there'll be no love from us passed to thee!"*

Our mother screamed in horror, but the spell had been cast. I could see as much in our father's face.

He walked over to Lance and backhanded him into the sunken living room. Lance staggered and fell, his head striking a glancing blow on the coffee table.

Blood poured from the head wound. Dad and Mom stood transfixed, while Kyle rushed toward our brother and placed one of our mother's prize pillow against the bleeding cut.

"Blood spilled, and the curses are cast, I... I cast a curse," Dad said, sounding dazed.

"Call 911," I cried, but neither of our parents moved. I rushed out of the room, knocking Mom to the side, and pulled the house phone off the receiver and dialed.

Neither parent came to the hospital. It was just us—Lance in the hospital bed, and Kyle and me waiting. The Department of Children's Services came by and got our story, well, most of it—not the part about the spells that'd been tossed about—just the part about us coming out, and our father knocking Lance into the living room. No, he didn't mean to hurt him, not to the point of hospitalization anyway, but that didn't discount the fact that he'd cursed us, then physically lashed out.

We sat silently staring at one another until our grandmother arrived. She was cheerful, with tie-dye skirts flowing around her ankles, smelling of roses, lavender, and happiness.

"Looks like I just inherited a trio of wayward youths! Well, get on with it. Lance, you okay to stand and walk?" she asked.

He nodded, then winced. "I'm fine, Grandma."

Despite her forced cheer, I could feel the pain she carried that day. That was the only time I'd ever seen my grandmother's joyful spirit dim. No, none of us were fine. She knew we weren't, but the woman was nothing if not full of hope. Before we got up, she leaned over my brother, and kissed him on the uninjured side of his head. "You will be, baby," she whispered. "I promise, you will be."

Chapter Two

Present Day: Crea

"Hey, you're the one who lives in Oregon," I responded, after Lance made some exasperated comment about me keeping him on the phone.

"Crea, I'm Attorney General…"

"And I'm running… you know what, it doesn't matter. I'm here. Are you sure you'll be able to get away? I'm taking a lot of time off to do this…" I said.

"It's not me you've got to worry about. You know how Kyle is."

I shook my head thinking about our baby brother. "Have you even spoken to him?" I asked, and Lance just laughed.

"Okay, that's a no. Well, text him or something, he listens to you more than me. I also think Crater Lake is a cool spot to meet, especially since it's where Grandma and Grandpa met. At least, according to Grandma's stories."

Lance was quiet, and I wasn't sure whether he was thinking about our grandmother, or just ignoring me like he usually did when I called.

"Okay, I'm about to hit a national forest, and there's never coverage in those. I'll Facetime you when I get to the park, and you can thumbs up or down our choices of staying around there."

"Thanks, brother... and yeah, I'll text Kyle... not that it'll do any good."

I smiled as I hung up. I didn't spend much time with my brothers, not like I should, but there was always this wall between us... a wall our dad had built. Despite that, I was determined to maintain some sort of connection, or at least try to.

I put my phone down, turned up my favorite CD since the national forests were notorious for poor radio reception, and cruised toward Crater Lake National Park. Hopefully, given Lance and Kyle both lived in Oregon, they'd be willing to join me there for a weekend of getting reunited.

It'd been two freaking years since I'd seen them, after all. Not to mention that our grandmother had passed away during that time. At the very least, they could spare their brother a weekend.

CHAPTER THREE

ELI

THE CANTILEVER BUCKED, AND I dropped it, causing the log to roll off the sawmill, knock me down, and roll right over my left leg. As I lay on the ground, pain searing through me, I chastised myself for not oiling the damned thing first thing that morning.

"Fuck," I said out loud, knowing nobody was gonna hear me anyway. I was out in the woods by myself, miles from anyone or anything.

As I lay trying to convince myself to get up, I saw the daytime moon and could feel her chuckling. "Okay, Goddess, I know you've been pushing me to get out and be social, but damn, did you have to do it this way?"

"Yes!" I could swear I heard her say, but then again, I could've been hallucinating. The pain was that intense.

No matter how bad I hurt now, though, I knew from experience it was going to hurt a lot more when I started moving.

I leaned up on my elbows, and immediately broke out into a cold sweat. "Fuck, I'm FUCKED!" I yelled, and lay back down.

My ATV was just over the ridge. I had to make it there or I'd be screwed for sure. My ranger buddy told me there'd been bear and cougar sightings just this week, in the very same spot I was working. On the ground, injured, I was a sitting duck!

I looked back at the moon and bit my tongue, resisting the sudden urge to call the Goddess some choice names I'd later regret.

I grabbed a piece of bark off the ground that I'd shaved off a log just moments before my big faux pas. I scooted up to the back of the sawmill, managing to reach around and turn the damned thing off. Then I bit down on the bark and pushed myself up onto my good foot.

Pain overwhelmed me.

I closed my eyes and waited for the world to right itself again. I couldn't afford to fall. I doubted I'd get back up. When I opened my eyes, I searched for anything that could help me keep my balance and prevent my crushed leg from flapping around as I ventured from the sawmill to the ATV. Everything was too short or too long. Finally, I found a stick that was a little too short to be much help, but I'd have to make it work at a crutch. I just needed to get to the vehicle.

I thought then that I should probably have figured out how to secure my leg, but damn, I was up and couldn't afford to stop the momentum. I needed to do this now.

I tried hopping, and *fuck*. My injured leg bumped against my other one and I saw stars, then stumbled. I landed on my good knee, but the pain in my left was so intense, I vomited all over the fucking stick I was using as a crutch.

Okay, Eli. Get it together, you've got this. I reached over, grabbed the stick, vomit and all, and stuck it behind my good leg. I took my shirt off and began tearing it into strips. Not too hard, the shirt was ancient and ripped easily. What sucked was that I loved that fucking shirt. I'd bought it at a Nirvana concert in ninety-four, one of their last.

Fuck it, I thought as I continued tearing, then managed to laugh at myself. My mom had lectured me the last time I'd gone to see her that I cussed too much. "Seems undignified and not how I taught you to be," she'd said. Maybe she had a valid point, but *fuck* if I cared right now.

I managed to tie the strips around my leg and the stick and got the fucking thing—*sorry, Mom*—to rest at the base of my ass and stick out low enough below my foot to allow me to use it as a fake leg.

"Goddess, make this work!" I demanded, no longer trying to show any respect. I fully blamed her for the mess I was in.

Thank all the heavens, it worked. The pain was intense, but not puking or seeing stars intense. I was able to gently stumble along using my support and the leg brace to get me over to the fucking ATV.

For good measure, when I sat down, I screamed *fuck* one more time.

I drew in a long, deep breath, and pulled my crushed leg up into the ATV. Thank the *gods* the vehicle was big enough that I could keep it straight and still rest it on the makeshift support.

I started the engine and slowly pushed down on the gas. It revved to life, and I jerked, not a lot, but enough to send stars shooting across my vision again.

I put the ATV back into park, closed my eyes, and waited a moment. *Find your center, Eli.* I allowed my mind to imagine the energy from the earth flowing into me through my legs and up my torso, then energy from the sky flowing into my head and down my body. Blue and green were the colors I saw in my mind's eye.

I waited while I let the energies fill me back up, and when I opened my eyes, I felt like I was going to be okay. I could do this.

I put the ATV back in gear and pushed down on the gas again. It still hurt like hell, but this time when it popped, I didn't see stars. Any improvement was welcome.

I drove as gently as I could, cussing loudly each time I hit a bump, no matter how slight, as the pain was immense.

I had no idea how, but I managed to get to the ranger's station, and prayed to all that was good and holy, someone would be in. The odds were not good, though, since the Feds had pulled more funding from the forestry service... again.

When I found it empty, I had to resist the urge to cry. *Fuck me!* I had managed the two-mile drive down the mountain, and as was my luck, still hadn't found any help. "You knew it was a long shot," I said out loud, then I lowered my head to the steering wheel and rested, hoping against hope, someone would come along.

I was getting tired, really fast. I knew a service station lay a mile down the road. Maybe that was a better choice. They were likely closed too, but if I could get there, I might get enough cell coverage to use my phone.

I gathered what little energy I had left, and wiped away the tear that escaped my eye. The pain only continued to ramp up as my excruciating nightmare continued.

I pulled onto the road, and got a third of a mile when my ATV began to sputter.

"No, hell no! What are you doing?" I yelled at the machine. "Why?" I looked up to where the moon should be. "Why are you doing this to me?"

I was met with silence as the ATV slowly drifted to a stop. I was so messed up I burst into tears, and didn't even care.

I had my head down when I heard a vehicle approach, speed past me, and judging by the sound of squeaking brakes, slowed down . Maybe they were coming back, but it hurt too much to look up. I was done. I figured either some passerby would help me or I'd die alone out here in the woods. It was still too cold for much tourist traffic, but I was on a main road now at least.

I heard the vehicle slow to a stop next to me and a window roll down. "Hey, you okay?" a guy asked.

I glanced up into a pair of soulful green eyes, but my mind was gone. The pain was too much, and I was going into shock.

"No, you're not, are you?" I could hear the alarm in his voice as he opened his car door and rushed over to me. "Hey, buddy, what's your name?" I could only manage a pained grunt in answer. "Okay, can you help me at all?" he asked, but I couldn't do much. When he put his arm under me, I tensed, and when my foot knocked against the ATV, I screamed and passed out.

Chapter Four

CREA

I ALMOST DIDN'T STOP. After hanging up with Lance, I'd left the interstate to check the outlying areas around Crater Lake in case my picky older brother was against us staying at any of the limited options within the park itself.

When I noticed the ATV, I was upset some jackass had left it sitting in the middle of the lane. When I darted around it, though, I saw out of the corner of my eye its driver was slumped over the steering wheel.

I slowed down, cussing under my breath, and pulled back around. "Hey, you okay?"

Even as I said the words, I could tell he wasn't. Shock, that was my guess, and the way his foot was secured to a branch indicated a messed-up leg. He needed help, and fast.

He wasn't responding to my questions as I went to help him up. Unfortunately, his leg or foot must have bumped the vehicle because he screamed, then passed out.

"Shit!" I said as I quickly grabbed the lumberjack of a man. He was huge. At least six five. His shirt was off, even though it was only fifty degrees if we were lucky. He was built, no doubt, but with a little pudge. I saw what looked to be his shirt had been used to support his injured leg.

I managed to drag him over to my rental, opened the back door, and all but shoved him in.

I hoped he didn't have any other injuries. If so, I probably just helped him with several internal bleeds. Couldn't be helped, though. All that man was more than I could handle gently.

When I got him into the back seat, I went to the other side, pulled his body up, and closed the door. I made sure his injured leg, which smelled a whole lot like puke, was well supported and out of the door's way when I shut it.

I was about to get in when I remembered his ATV was still in the middle of the road. I doubted there would be much traffic this time of year, but the least I could do was push it onto the shoulder. I went over, put the thing in neutral, and pushed it well off the road, then reached over and took the keys.

I didn't have good cell coverage and I had no idea what was in the direction of the park, but I damned well knew there wasn't anything else between here and the town I'd driven through to get here. If he was going to make it to a hospital, it was going to have to be me that got him there.

"Hey, buddy," I said several times, but the man behind me didn't move. "Damn, you really need to wake up, buddy. I'm not trained to do much other than rush you to the hospital, but I'm sure you're not supposed to stay unconscious."

I kept talking to him the entire time it took to get back to the town and to find the hospital. I pulled into the Emergency Department, checked on the guy, and seeing he was still alive at least, I rushed through the automatic doors. "I need help here!"

A woman behind the front desk looked up, clearly startled by my yelling.

"I found a guy on the side of the road, half-dead. He's unconscious in my back seat. I need help getting him out."

She called out for help, and the department went into action. Within a few moments, a man and woman with a gurney raced out of a back room toward my waiting car.

They managed to ease the man out of my back seat and onto the gurney, and then disappeared inside with him.

I was about to get in my car and leave when a security guard approached and asked me to come inside.

I was taken into a small room, and shortly after a guy announcing himself as an RN joined us.

"Can you tell us how you found this guy?" the nurse asked.

"Sure, I was driving through the national forest toward Crater Lake, somewhere close to Diamond Lake, I think. I saw an ATV sitting in the road and as I drove by, I noticed him slumped in the driver's seat..."

When I'd finished the story, the nurse nodded. "I'm going to go check on him again. Tim here will get your personal information. I'm sure the sheriff will want to chat with you, so can you stay here a few more minutes?"

I shrugged. "Sure." I just need to move my car. I left it out front."

"It'll be fine," Tim, the security guard, said. "I'll call over to the sheriff's office, and if they don't need you, you can go."

I leaned back in the chair, and waited for the two men to come back and let me know whether I could go.

It took a lot longer than I'd anticipated. I'd only had a few hours' sleep the night before, and I managed to drift off. When the door opened, I woke with a start.

"Sorry," I said as the nurse came back in. "You'd think I'd be able to stay awake with this much excitement, huh?"

He smiled. "The sheriff's office said they didn't need you for anything, but the guy is awake and asked to see you."

"Me?" I asked. "Are you sure? He only glanced at me before he passed out."

The nurse shrugged, and I followed him through the Emergency Department and into a cubicle surrounded by curtains.

"Hi," I said as the guy whose name I still didn't know lay sprawled out on the bed.

He tried to smile at me, but I could see how much pain he was in. "Thank you," he said. "I don't know what I'd have done if you hadn't come by."

I nodded and almost patted his shoulder before I thought I'd better not, since I didn't know what parts of him were hurt.

He noticed and said, "Just the leg."

I nodded, and the nurse came up behind me. "Mr. Bane, we need to take you to x-ray."

The nurse began to wheel him out of the room when he turned to me and said in a weak voice, "Wait, can you leave your information with the hospital? I'd like to thank you properly."

I could tell the conversation was taking a lot out of him, as his handsome face, shaped by a well-manicured beard, went from a perfect bronze to a definite shade of green.

"Sure, man, I'm happy to. Oh, I have your ATV key, too. I'll leave that with them as well."

He nodded, and then he was gone.

I did as he asked. I walked to the front desk and left my name, my San Francisco address, and almost left my phone number but stopped, silently chastising myself. *What are you doing trying to hook up with a guy who crushed his leg?*

The woman smiled and put the paper with my contact details and ATV key I'd pulled out of my pocket into a small manila envelope that had the guy's name on it. *Eli Bane.*

Good, at least I had a name to go with the handsome face. I was sure HIPAA wouldn't be too keen on the fact she'd accidentally given that to me, but who was I to tell?

I crawled back into my rental, sighed when the earthy smell of the lumberjack hit me, then cringed when the pleasant aroma was mixed with the smell of vomit. "Sorry, sexy lumberjack," I said to myself as I pulled out from under the awning. "I'm gonna have to Febreze you away. Vomit isn't something I wanna be smelling for the next few hundred miles."

I found a supermarket, bought some Febreze, wet wipes, and a cup of coffee, and freshened up the smell before turning the car back toward Crater Lake.

Chapter Five

Eli

I WOKE UP TO a very frustrated Lee Chelsea looking at me. He had his arms crossed, and it looked like if he pursed his lips together any harder, his face would collapse in on itself.

"Just what I wanted to see after waking up from surgery," I said as the man came and stood over me.

"Want to explain to me how you almost ended up bear meat on top of the pass?" he asked. I could tell that my friend, the retired ranger, was livid.

I closed my eyes again and willed him to disappear.

"Oh no, you aren't going to sleep again until I get an explanation why you were up on that hill by your damned self."

Just then, I heard a nurse come in and tell Lee he needed to let me rest.

"The hell I will. Can't you see how close he came to being killed up there?"

"Yes," she replied. "But it won't do him any good to chastise him right now. He needs to rest and recuperate. You can yell at him about being stupid later."

I opened my eyes again and noticed the nurse was Lee's daughter, Libby. "No fair, this is two against one," I managed to say.

Both chuckled, and Lee gently put his hand on my shoulder. "You scared the shit out of all of us, boy, and you do have hell to pay for that. But Libby's right, you need to rest. And just so you know, I'm gonna pick you up as soon as they let you out of here, and you're staying with us."

I started to protest, and stopped when I saw the look both he and his daughter were giving me. "Damn, the two of you have the same evil, 'don't sass me' look."

Libby chuckled. Lee didn't.

"I don't care where you put me," I said, closing my eyes and drifting back off.

When I woke up, the room was empty, and I was grateful for that. I was afraid of the inevitable lecture I was gonna get from Lee.

I tried sitting up. Thankfully, they must have decreased the pain medication, because I didn't feel like I was going to pass out again.

However, I quickly changed my mind when I sat up further and felt my leg resist me. "Fuck," I hissed.

"It's gonna hurt for a while," Libby said as she walked in. "Want more pain pills? You're due for another one."

I shook my head. "Give me a minute to find out what I can and can't handle, but then, yeah, I'll want it."

Libby came over and helped me sit up properly, putting a pillow behind me for support.

I lay back, amazed at just how worn out I was from the effort.

"You did quite a number on that leg. It's almost like you were trying to see how many pieces you could break it into," Libby said.

Bitchy much, I thought, but kept it to myself.

Despite my love of solitude, I'd gotten to know the Chelsea family, at the gatherings in Chemeketa. It was always hard for me to socialize. Not that there was anything wrong with me, I just preferred solitude and being alone with nature.

The great old-growth forests around Chemeketa resonated with me. Every year when my family arrived at our designated hut overlooking the river, I'd disappear into the great woods and often didn't return until I heard my mom's voice in my head telling me it was time to leave. It wasn't unusual for me to miss the entire event.

Of course, my parents insisted I attend a few of them, but my great-grandfather had told them when I was born not to intervene too much. I was destined to be in the forests, he'd said, and it was important that I be allowed to grow and nourish myself there.

It was one of my most fervent wishes that he could've lived long enough for me to know him properly. Unfortunately, he died when I was only two, too young to develop enough of a bond to even conjure up his image during one of my scrying spells.

Apparently, I'd grown quiet because Libby placed her hand on my shoulder. "Are you dreaming of being back in the forest?" she asked.

I laughed. "I have to admit, it was more about you and how we didn't really hang out much at the Chemeketa ceremonies."

She just shrugged. "You're earth, I'm air..." As if that explained everything.

"Is your husband an air energy?" I asked, already knowing the answer.

"Hardly," she chuckled. "The man was made to have his hands in the earth." Finally, she realized what I was getting at and shook her head.

"You know, some of us are so controlled and inspired by our elemental sign, it's hard to connect to anyone who isn't. Luckily, that's not the case with me and lucky, too, since as you know, both of my parents are about as earth centric as someone can be."

She walked around, tending to the bed, and making sure all my tubes were working. "You were always very intensely... earth. We all knew that was just you."

I shrugged. "You're right, in that forests are very earth based. Living in McMinnville, the only forests were the ones that were harvested year after year. The old-growth spoke to me on a different level. Getting back to Chemeketa and seeing the trees was like visiting an old friend. I spent so much time with them, I seldom had time to visit with the humans."

Libby chuckled. "It's all good. Weird as it may be, it isn't that weird for our..."–she hesitated for a moment– "...well, our people. Okay, now about that pain pill. Now or later?"

"Now, definitely now!" I said, the pain slowly kicking up. "Can you use some of that air energy to help make me a little less uncomfortable?" I blushed at the question. I never asked for help... and that went double for asking for that kind of help, but after lying in this bed for so long, I need a bit more than a pain pill.

She chuckled, and after checking the door of my room was closed, came over next to the bed. She chanted words I wasn't able to hear, and just like that, it felt like I was lying on a bed of air. "That should help," she said, then winked at me before she left to get the pill.

After taking it, I said, "Night night," knowing it would only take a few moments to kick in.

She smiled. "I'll check back in on you before I end my shift. Oh, and just so you know, I think you'll be discharged tomorrow. Dad's already planning to pick you up."

I rolled my eyes. "Your dad thinks I'm still a teenager."

She looked sad. "He thinks you still need a surrogate dad. It does him good though, so you let him keep it up."

I nodded. When my mom and dad passed away, Lee Chelsea stepped up to the plate. I was already over eighteen, but he and Dad had been close, and the story went that he was my de facto parent if anything happened to one of mine.

It worked well for me since Lee was a ranger for the national forests around Crater Lake. After my parents' funeral, I'd moved closer to him, and I'd been there ever since.

Lee was at the hospital by nine, and I was discharged shortly after. I hobbled out on the stupid crutches, refusing to be pushed in their even-more stupid chair. The whole 'We have to for liability reasons' comment from the orderly who was determined to get me in the chair got a 'Tell your attorney to shove it up his ass' response from me. Regardless, the aide followed me down the hallway, from the time I hobbled out of the room, until I got into Lee's truck.

"Damn, you'd think by the way he was determined to get me in that chair, they hadn't traipsed my ass up and down the halls for the last forty-eight hours. Libby herself forced me out of bed shortly after surgery," I said, getting a chuckle from Lee.

"So, why is it you think I can't take care of myself?" I asked, then moaned inwardly at my stupidity. I'd just opened the door for Lee to nail me again.

The older man looked at me, and as if he could read my mind, smiled. "Wanna tell me why you were out there with faulty equipment without backup?" he asked. When I didn't respond, he laughed. "Well, I guess we can both have our secrets, huh?"

The conversation then drifted to my latest job. I was hoping to acquire a few hardwood logs that had been discarded when the last load was cut up on the pass. These particular logs were gnarly as shit, and perfect for turning the parts I wanted for my most recent sculpture.

"You've seen the logs I brought down, so you already know what I've got from up there. Hell, I still can't believe they toss those beauties to the side and burn them."

"They don't see the same value in them that you do. Hell, I'd just cut them up for firewood myself, and with all those damned knots, they'd be a pain to split even with the electric splitter." He smiled when I made a face. "Son, I know it's hard for you to understand, but most anyone would toss those logs aside."

I just shook my head. We'd had this debate before. The more difficult the log, the more intense the sculpture. A plain log with no imperfections led to boring works of art. I was also a big supporter of ending logging as we knew it. Humans wasted the wood anyway. We all knew we needed to let the old-growth forests come back, heal the atmosphere, decrease carbon, and have a cool place to hang out, all at the same time.

I wasn't going to win that argument with Lee, so I didn't even try. He believed trees could and should be grown like crops, which was basically what he oversaw with the US Forest Service.

I drifted off before we got back to Lee's place. It was truly amazing how much my body needed to rest. Of course, I knew I was still healing, and that took a lot of energy, but it was still frustrating. It sucked that I'd have to spend so much time recuperating. Hell, there'd be so many tourists swarming around by the time I got back to the job site, I was sure I'd have a hell of a time pulling logs out and more likely than not, several of them would have messed with my mill.

"Fuck," I said out loud as I remembered my mill.

"What?" Lee said, concerned.

"I forgot my damned sawmill is still up on the pass."

"Nope, it's back in your workshop along with your ATV. The boys and I loaded it all up and moved it there while you were laid up in the hospital," he chuckled.

"Trust me, I'd have much rather been out there with y'all."

"I know, son, but at least we were able to get it all tucked away."

"Lucky for me, I can still get up there and get my logs pulled before the snows hit again," I said.

"No need, unless you wanted more than the ones you had stacked up next to the sawmill. We brought those down too. Ria pulled those down on her old logging truck and her husband Sam was able to load them with his forklift. It ain't like they were that big, after all."

"Big enough." I patted the cast on my leg.

Lee looked over and shook his head. "It was stupid to be up there without help. I know you have a zone you get in, but as you've learned, the unexpected is always lurking. Besides, it's high time you had an apprentice. You're not getting any younger, and you know the code. You're to pass on the knowledge to the younger crowd."

I moaned. The same lecture had been coming at me off and on for the past decade. So far, I hadn't met anyone who could be an apprentice, and I sure wasn't going to pluck some self-indulgent twenty-year-old out of the air.

I tried not to think about how the moon had shone down on me, or that I'd believed it was all part of some conspiracy to get me out of the woods. I'd forgotten about the code, and my promise to bring on an apprentice when Lee had taken me in all those years back. Damn, had I brought this on myself?

I concentrated on the road ahead, getting the thoughts out of my head. No, the Goddess didn't break people's legs like a damned Mob boss. Over the years, there were some who'd come to believe that, but not me. Not most of those who practiced.

It would've been more likely that I'd have lost my inspiration, or lost the skills I'd acquired after joining the Chemeketa Earth Guild. Lost what I'd promised to uphold, like a parent who believed in letting their children learn through natural consequences. All that being said, there was no doubt in my mind that the Goddess wanted me out of the woods. Although she wasn't directly behind the breaking of my leg, she was going to take advantage of me while I was out.

CHAPTER SIX

CREA

I MANAGED TO GET back to San Francisco in one piece. I'd toured Crater Park with no other incidents after dropping the giant lumberjack off at the hospital.

My grandparents had met and fallen in love at Crater Lake National Park in the nineteen sixties. My brothers and I had talked repeatedly about going there before Grandma had died, so we could all go down to Chemeketa to visit her afterward. But there were always other parks more interesting—Yosemite, the Grand Canyon, the Great Smoky Mountains, just to name a few.

We had to work hard to make the time to see one another, and typically only had one week, or more often a weekend, at a time to spend together. I was determined that our family get-togethers happened, as they were as important to our well-being as a healthy diet. Well, maybe more so. We'd all three come to the same conclusion, probably because of the curses from way back, that we somehow needed to reconnect in real life to rejuvenate.

My father's curse had been true. None of us had developed long-term relationships with a man. My longest had ended a few months back. Donald was everything I wasn't. He was carefree, lighthearted, gregarious, and a total asshole when we were alone. I was timid and shy in public and opened my heart completely in private.

My brothers and niece had hated him. They'd only met a few times, but none of them liked him, and the feeling was mutual. When he finally left, he hurled that fact at me, saying it was my family's fault that we couldn't make a go of it.

Of course, he never took responsibility for his abusive nature when we were alone.

I sighed. *Okay, enough of that.* It didn't work out because I had a deep affinity for men who wanted to hurt me. I don't know if that's the curse—*okay, yes, I know it's the curse*—but it just feels like I can't date good men. I'm only attracted to the mean, nasty ones, or players.

I called my boss and told her I was back in town and could begin the process of setting up the urban gardens I helped to manage, then settled into my little bungalow by unpacking and pouring myself a glass of the wine I'd picked up while in Oregon.

Maybe if we had time, my brothers and I could go up to the wine country and tour a few vineyards. It was amazing how Oregon was giving California a run for their money with their wines these days. Some of the bottles I brought back with me were delicious.

Wine was around when we were growing up in Chemeketa, but it didn't seem to have the same resonance it did now, and since I'd left shortly after turning twenty-one, I hadn't had much time to try the wines out anyway. Hell, in the nineteen nineties, when my friends and I were running around, it was beer and wine coolers that ruled our parties. I hadn't discovered how much I liked wine until I was in my thirties.

It was still cool enough this time of year that I decided to light the fireplace. Not for the first time, I lamented it wasn't a wood-burning fireplace, but with San Francisco's fire restrictions, it didn't seem worth the effort, so I'd installed gas logs shortly after moving in.

The combination of fire and wine, along with exhaustion from driving day in and day out, weighed on me, and before I knew it, I was asleep.

The fog drifted across the road, and I immediately realized I was back where I'd found the injured man. I looked to the side and saw my father. Not his face, I could never see his face in my dreams, but I could tell he was angry.

"No son of mine is going to be with another man," I heard him say, and I shuddered. Those were the words he'd said before he cursed us to loneliness for the rest of our lives.

I looked across the street and could see my grandmother. I could tell she was angry at my father by the way she stared at him. Seeing her, even with the grimace she wore when she spoke of him and what he'd done to us, made me miss her. Losing her last fall was hard on all three of us.

"Grandma," I said, and she turned toward me. "Are you really here?"

She smiled and came over to embrace me.

"I'm here for now. Oh, and you've found the key to undoing the curse, I see."

"I have?" I asked, looking down at my hands for a key. When I didn't see one, I began to look around me.

"You were always so literal," Grandma chuckled.

When I looked back up at her, she waved her hand across the fog, and like a mystic television, images of the day I found the man with the busted leg flashed before me.

"He's the key?" I asked.

She smiled and shook her head. "Not just him, but what you and he can have together if you're able to work it out."

I dared to look at my father, but he was surrounded by the mist, and I could only make out his silhouette.

"He won't allow it," I said, feeling tears burn the backs of my eyes.

"This isn't his choice," she said bitterly, and flashed the vision away. "All things have a balance. He might have cursed you, but then his curse was returned. Yin and Yang always play their parts. Nothing will stop love forever, except apathy or lack of interest. Of the three of you, your heart is the strongest. It yearns for love in a way your brothers never have. It is, therefore, your place to start the dominoes falling."

"Grandma, I've tried. I keep failing. The men I fall for are never what they seem."

"That's why this one was brought to you, why you found him. That's the Goddess's way to rewrite your destiny."

I shook my head. "I don't understand. You're saying I can undo the curse, but only with this man?"

"No, dear one. I'm saying you had a good man put in your path to help you. The curse can't chase him away *or blind you to him, because he was put there for you to find."*

"You're saying the Goddess struck him in the leg so he could find me?" I asked, horrified.

She chuckled. "No, that's not how this works. He did that on his own. She just set it up so the two of you would cross paths."

"So, what am I supposed to do, go find him and kiss him like in one of those old movies you used to watch?"

She just shook her head, slipping her arm in mine like she'd done when I was a teenager. "No, my love, he will come to you. It's up to you to open your heart and help him open his. It won't be an easy task, but it's the only way for you to overcome."

Remembering how this worked, I sighed. "How much of this dream will I remember?"

She smiled at me. "You're learning. You will not remember much, just the part where you saw me and your father, and the memory of the injured man. But I'll be back. I'll be guiding you as you move forward. You have a major battle on your hands. Your father's curse is strong, just like he was when he cast it. It'll take all your strength to overcome it."

I sighed and sat down on the ground. "Grandma, I've never been strong."

She shook her head. "That's not true. You've always been strong enough, and have survived every trial you've faced throughout your life. The men who have been driven your way as a result of your father's curse have done what they could to destroy you, and although parts of you have been damaged as a result, like a war-

rior, you've survived. Don't underestimate your inner strength, my love."

"So, it's up to me to break the curse?"

She looked sad. "No, it's something each of you will have to overcome in your own way. I've left you something, however. You must return to my home and collect it. The stone that represents your life, it'll help ward off those who would undermine your spirit."

"Will I remember that?" I asked.

She nodded. "I'm allowed to leave one direction for you to follow. That is the one I leave you with."

She kissed me on my forehead like she always had when I was young, and pulling me up, she embraced me. "Your destiny is in your hands, dear one. Now, go take it by the horns!"

She walked toward where my father was standing, and as she neared his silhouette, they both disappeared into the fog.

Chapter Seven

Eli

RECOVERY WAS SLOW AND painful. Oh, and it itched to hell and back. If I could've clawed my cast off, there were times I'm sure I would've. Some earth energies had the ability to make vines grow. More than once I wished I had that kind of power... a good vine growing in my cast to scratch at all the itchy places would be very helpful about now.

The only thing that kept my mind at ease was my work. I ended up having to find help 'cause, frankly, I couldn't saw the wood myself, and I was damned sure not going to let my work languish because of my stupid leg.

I reached out to my connections, including my cousin in McMinnville and a couple of art schools interested in my work.

Finally, since the Goddess was all up in this, I decided to send my notice of apprentice to the folks who ran the Chemeketa Grange and meeting house. Maybe that would satisfy my obligation for an apprentice, and then when my leg healed, I could get on with my life.

The inquiries were endless. It gave me a headache going through them all. Too eager, too in your face, too social. Some sent videos of themselves attempting to do art with wood. One even said he was a younger version of me. I laughed when I saw that one, and said, "I hope not, kid."

I shouldn't have been surprised. My art had taken off shortly after I'd made it public. I had my cousin to blame for that. He displayed it in his winery, and several of his snooty patrons picked a few pieces up. Since then, I'd been plagued with people wanting to buy my work or interview me. I declined the interviews, and let my cousin, who was always much better at managing business stuff, price and sell my work. Of course, ever the businessman, he took a hefty chunk off the top, but because of him, I had a nice nest egg that included the monies I'd gotten from selling the farm and vineyard to him.

I ended up throwing all the damned apprentice applications in the trash. Nope, not interested! I could wait, I decided.

After tossing them all, a late submission caught my attention. Interestingly enough, it was from a young woman from New York City of all places.

She didn't really send me much about herself, other than her great-grandmother was from Chemeketa, and while visiting her friend there, she'd seen the notification I'd put out for an apprentice.

What stood out from the other applications was the tiny, beautifully carved raccoon she'd mailed with the required paperwork.

No formal training, no desire to become famous or be the next Eli Bane, and none of the other nonsense the kids had tried using to woo me. Just this little carving that seemed to perfectly capture the ornery, sweet nature of the animal itself.

Jennie Lambert seemed to be perfect. *Now to meet her and see for myself.* I contacted her and asked if she could meet me at my workshop for an interview. If I liked her, I'd let her stay in the little room behind the workshop I used when I got too wrapped up in what I was doing and needed to crash for a few hours. It was far from perfect accommodations, but if she really wanted to learn from me, she'd have to be okay with roughing it.

As fate would have it, as I was fully aware the universe was playing me, Jennie was still visiting her friend in Chemeketa. She drove down to meet me, and the connection between us was instant.

She was truly my opposite, bubbly, full of energy, and she talked a mile a minute. When the introductions were over, however, I watched her as she wandered among the different raw materials. She fell silent as she pondered the logs, touching them and running her hand across the imperfections as if she wanted to tease out whatever was lurking beneath the rough surface.

It could all be for show, however, so I pulled her application out, and said, "You don't have much experience. What makes you think you're qualified for this type of work?"

She looked over at me and shrugged. "I'm not really. My degree was going to be marketing and communication, but now I've decided to learn hands-on, and I've found I prefer to be in nature. I was hoping that by working with you, I'd... become qualified."

She never stopped touching the wood as she talked. Her honesty was refreshing, and wondering if this would be the part where I'd lose her, I asked, "So, have you seen my art before?"

She looked worried, then shook her head. "No, I'm sorry. I'm not from this part of the country."

I almost laughed out loud, but held it in. I'd had art displayed in some of the most prestigious galleries and museums in the country. I had the Metropolitan Museum of Art begging me to do a commission for years before I finally accepted. It was broadcast in *The New York Times*. I didn't give a shit about all that, but it seemed weird this girl didn't know about it if she loved woodworking as much as she said she did.

I decided to take her into my finishing workshop and see if she showed any signs of recognition. We walked into the room, and Jennie gasped and rushed to the table with the piece I was currently working on. She immediately reached out, then pulled her hand back, and walked around the piece staring at the different details. I would've been impressed if I wasn't suspicious.

When she came to the part that I always did, the little twizzle, as I called it, her eyes lit up, and she gasped again. "Eli Bane, you're *the* Eli Bane," she said, and shook her head. "Oh, I'm an idiot."

She sat down on the little stool I had sitting next to the piece, the one I used when sanding or polishing.

She put her hand on top of her head. "Well, this isn't going to work," she said, and stood up. "I'm sorry I wasted your time, Mr. Bane." And she walked toward the door.

"Wait, why have you wasted my time?" I asked.

"I'm Linda Lambert's daughter." She watched me as recognition dawned and shook her head, walking toward the door again.

"Hey," I yelled. "I can't chase you. I've got a bum leg here, remember?" It was too late, she was gone. *Well, how do you like that?*

Linda Lambert was a hot-shot freelance art critic and reporter who'd been harassing me since the art museum had commissioned my piece. She'd done everything except show up at my door. Being suspicious, I might have thought this was her way to finally get an interview, sending her daughter to my workshop as an apprentice candidate, but everything in me said that wasn't the case. Jennie had accidentally stumbled onto me, and now she was running away, probably afraid I was going to yell at her.

I chuckled to myself. Thumbing through my phone, I found her mom's number from the last email she'd sent.

"Hello, is this Linda Lambert?" I asked.

"No, this is her husband. How can I help you?"

"Hi, I'm Eli Bane. Linda has been trying to get me to sit for an interview. Your daughter just left my workshop and I'd like to find out if Linda sent her here."

"Wait, what? Jennie just sat for an interview with you? For what?" he asked.

Well, that helped confirm it wasn't deliberate.

"That's what I'm trying to ascertain," I responded. "Was her interest in applying real, or just another ploy from her mother to get an interview with me?"

The guy sighed. "Our daughter isn't part of anything we do professionally. I'm sorry if you think we were using her to get to you, but if she sat for an interview with you, it was because whatever she was applying for is important to her. I'll let Linda know you called, but please be assured, we don't want anything about our lives to impede Jennie's aspirations."

I liked the man immediately. Maybe I'd reconsider the interview with his wife after all, even though she was known for being cutting and direct. I didn't want to be interviewed by anyone, and sure as hell not someone who liked to slash and burn artists. Although that might not be a fair assessment of her, since everything I'd ever read by her was spot on, and I agreed with her assessments, no matter how direct and painful they might've been to the artist.

"Can you please let Jennie know I'm still interested? And I would like her to return for a full interview. I promise not to hold her mother's profession against her."

I wanted to laugh when the guy spluttered. I could hear the emotion when he responded, "Thank you, Mr. Bane."

About thirty minutes later, Jennie knocked on my door. When she walked in, I could tell she'd been crying. I felt for her. I knew her mom was famous nationwide, and I couldn't imagine how she was regarded in New York. Some circles probably saw Jennie as a pariah, while others worshiped her. Both could make a child's life a living hell.

"Listen, I'm not really interested in an interview," I said, and Jennie immediately opened her mouth like she was going to respond. "Before you say anything, if I thought you were here for any other reason than to be my apprentice, this would've been over before it started. I haven't met your mother, though, so let's be very clear, you are not to be a go-between for her and me. I won't be pushed in that direction, even if that isn't your intention now. If I take you on, you'll have to keep your mom's agenda out of my life. Are we clear?"

Jennie nodded. "In her defense, she's never tried to use me to better her career. I doubt she would now. In fact, if I'm working for you, it might give you a break from her relentless pressure to interview with her."

I laughed. "You're selling yourself as a way to get your mom off my back?"

The young woman's face turned scarlet, and before she could leave again, I laughed. "Jennie, you've got the job if you want it, but it's a lot of hard work, and the accommodations are less than ideal. I'll let you go back and see them before you give me an answer."

She looked at me dumbfounded. "Really, you're hiring me?" she asked. "I thought you were going to yell at me or something. I-I didn't expect you to offer me the job. You know I don't have any woodworking experience, right?"

I chuckled. "When did you make the raccoon?"

She looked embarrassed. "I made him while I was visiting my friend in Chemeketa. The woods there are just so..." She hesitated and looked at her feet.

"They are enchanted," I said, finishing the thought for her.

She looked up and nodded.

"I've always felt the same way. I used to go up there every summer with my family, and I'd peruse the old-growth forests that line the coast. I carved my first piece there when I was only eight years old."

Jennie smiled. "I've gotten a little later start."

"Ah, well, it isn't your fault. It's not like you had a lot of forests in New York City."

She chuckled and nodded. "Mr. Bane, I don't care if I have to sleep on the ground. I'm all about working with you if you'll have me."

"Then, it's settled. If you take your stuff back and change into some work clothes, we can get started now."

I showed her to the apartment, if you could call it that, and gave her a key so she could lock up and feel secure when alone. I loved the seclusion, but I'd guess coming from the city, it'd be rather disconcerting to be out here alone at night.

When Jennie emerged, we sat down for a cup of tea, and talked about what she knew about power tools. As I suspected, it was nothing, but she was sure she wasn't afraid of them. She'd used her great-grandmother's chainsaw when she'd visited as a kid, and said she did fine with it.

I decided to work with her on using some of the more basic power tools before we graduated to the sawmill, although that was what I needed help with the most. Maybe I'd see if Lee could come out tomorrow and help her, since that would be her first time running it.

She was a natural on the saws and precise measuring each cut, and when I presented her with a problem requiring mathematical skills to figure out the proper cuts, she was able to do most of the calculating in her head. "You were good in geometry," I chuckled after a particularly difficult one.

She blushed. "No, not really. I'm more of a hands-on person, but when you put something in front of me, like these angles, I can usually figure it out without all the theorems and equations."

I nodded, impressed. "I never did very well with book mathematics either, but could figure most equations out when it came to woodworking." I'd often wondered why math teachers just didn't put their students in a workshop and ask them to figure it out on their own.

By the time evening arrived, both Jennie and I were exhausted. My leg had started giving me problems shortly after we started, and I'd resisted taking another damned pain pill so I could spend time working with her, but by five o'clock I was done.

Lee came by then to check on me. One look, and he said playtime was over. I just shook my head and told him to meet Jennie, my new apprentice.

That shocked him, but he recovered quick enough and grabbed Jennie's hand. "I never thought he'd ever hire one. You must be pretty special," he said to her.

"Yeah, yeah, she is, and you can get to know all about it," I interjected. "Meanwhile, I need to get back to the pain pills. Do you mind if Jennie joins us tonight for dinner? She can have mine. I'm almost certain I'm only going to be good for bed this evening."

"Yes, she can join us, and no, you'll not be avoiding a meal. You know Libby told you taking those pills on an empty stomach can make you feel awful, but we can get something in you quick enough. Jennie, why don't you leave your car here? I'll drive you back after dinner."

She nodded. I could tell she was skeptical of the arrangement. I hadn't told her I was hurting, and her expression said she was concerned about me. I wasn't one to be coddled. Hopefully, she'd understand that soon enough.

Lee's wife, Indigo, and Libby and her husband, Jake, all met us as we walked into the house. Indigo handed me a sandwich, which I ate without argument, then Libby came out of my room with the bottle of pain pills and handed me one. "You should've taken this three hours ago, and you shouldn't be out working this soon after you got out of the hospital."

"Yes, Mother," I replied, giving her a nasty look.

She smirked at me. "You really are as stubborn as Dad says you are."

"Nope, I'm probably worse, but do you think your father and I could have been friends this long if we didn't both stand toe to toe in stubbornness?" I asked.

"Hey," Lee said behind me. "I haven't been stubborn in at least a year. Ain't that right, Indigo, my dearest?"

She just laughed and walked into the kitchen. I'd known the woman as long as I had Lee, and she wasn't one for idle conversation. She was a woman of few words. I respected and liked that about her. Lee was more like Jennie, gregarious and full of life. The two seemed to fit like a glove.

Luckily *and* unfortunately, the medication kicked in quickly. I ended up saying goodbye to Jennie and setting up to see her the next day, then heading for the little bedroom off the back of the house, I turned in for the night.

It really was perfect for me. The room was octagonal with windows on each side, except for the one that led into the house. I had my own bathroom just outside that doorway, so I didn't have to hop or hobble too far.

The surrounding forest grew right up against the house. I could look out the windows and almost feel like I was in amongst the trees again. I'd loved this part of the house when Lee had built it. I'd even helped him with a few of the design elements, not that he needed them, he was my mentor after all.

Lee could've been a carpenter, furniture builder, contractor, or artist like me, but where I loved turning the wood into sculpture, he just loved the wood. He was an advocate of logging, which I never understood, but at the same time, he was as in love with the old-growth forests in the national park and along the coast as I was.

After I lost my parents, he and I took a week-long trip to Redwood National and State Parks, just across the Oregon border in California, and spent the entire time hiking through the incredible giants. That, more than anything, helped me deal with my parents' passing.

I fell asleep looking out into Lee's forest. The dream came on in an instant.

I was standing in the middle of a great clear-cut on the mountain. The immediate impact of seeing so many trees cut down in their prime hit me hard, but it was a feeling I was accustomed to. No matter how used to it I became, it still felt like stumbling on a murder scene.

There was a fog creeping among the stumps, and it was neither friendly nor embracing like the fogs I'd come to look forward to along the Oregon Coastal Range.

This fog was menacing, and I could tell it carried a threat.

I wanted to run, but when I tried, I was stuck in place. I looked down at my legs, and they were tree trunks grown into the ground. The fog continued rolling until it overtook me, and I could feel it fighting to get inside me. I held my breath until my lungs were screaming for air. I opened my eyes just in time to see a small older woman with flowing tie-dye clothes stepping out into the fog. Her presence immediately forced it to shrink back. As she waved her large staff, made of Oak and adorned with all sorts of stones and crystals, the fog began to dissipate. When it had completely disappeared, the woman turned to look at me. The stern look she'd held when driving the fog away morphed into a mischievous grin. She looked me up and down, then said, "Well, shit, you are hot as fuck, aren't you?"

At the woman's words, I startled awake in a cold sweat with my head throbbing.

I could still feel the invasiveness of the fog trying to force its way inside me and trying to suffocate me at the same time. I could also feel the gentle, sweet spirit of the woman who'd driven it away. It almost felt like I'd met her before. There was certainly something familiar about her that I couldn't quite put my finger on.

I shook off the dream, figuring it was definitely prophetic, but often dreams could be altered by using strong drugs. I'd definitely need to keep my eyes open in case the fog represented a real threat. Still, I had a feeling the little old woman represented my protector and advocate.

I looked over at my clock and cussed. Ten a.m., and I was still in bed. *Fuck,* I was supposed to meet Jennie.

I rushed to pull some clothes on when I heard voices. In the kitchen, Jennie and Lee were sitting at the counter, looking over several magazines. When I came closer, I saw they were looking at pictures of my work that had been published.

"Where did you get all these," I asked Lee.

He looked up and smiled. "I kept them," he said, reaching over to pull out the magazine that showed my piece in the Metropolitan Museum. "This is one of my favorites. Can you see how the texture changes in the different pieces of wood? It almost looks like it's alive."

"I've seen this one in person," she said, and ran her finger over the picture, almost like she had to the wood in the workshop. "It begs to be touched, but if you do, the guards get really pissed off."

I laughed. "I'm guessing you know that firsthand?"

She blushed. "I'm a tactile learner," she said. "It's both my biggest fault and greatest asset, or so I've been told."

"Luckily for you, there'll be a lot of hands-on learning, and there'll be no guards to piss off in the workshop."

She smiled. "You feeling better this morning?" she asked.

I looked at her for a moment. "Don't you be worrying about that. I'll take care of myself. You do the same. Okay?"

She looked properly chastised, and Lee patted her back. "Don't worry, he's a major pain in the ass when he's down, like an injured bear, but it's okay to keep an eye on him. His bark is worse than his bite... almost."

Jennie just looked down at the picture, not knowing what to say.

"Speaking of needing something, I need something for a headache. I slept too hard last night and had a wicked dream, something to do with fog and a crazy old woman in tie-dye."

Jennie stared at me with a bewildered look, and although I thought she wanted to say something, she held her tongue. That would bode well for her. I didn't do well with people trying to interpret my dreams. Hell, I tried not to myself.

After I'd medicated my headache with coffee and pills, I had Lee help me wrap my cast and got into the shower to let the hot water pour over my head. By the time I was finished, I felt almost like I was going to be able to make it through the day.

Lee went out to the workshop with us to help Jennie learn the sawmill. While they worked together, I focused on my current piece.

Since being rescued by the mystery man after my leg was crushed, I kept envisioning the sculpture I was working on resting in his hands. I'd almost decided to add his hands to it, but the more I thought about it, I realized the piece needed his actual hands on it, not an addition to the sculpture.

I'd been rather obsessed with him. *Creagan Franklyn.* I knew his name and address from the note he'd left for me at the hospital, but I only had glimpses of him in my mind's eye. His eyes were the thing I remembered most, vivid green, and his hands. I kept seeing visions of his hands, big and wide, but not as big as mine. There was something almost feminine about him, slender and smooth, but nothing definitive since I'd only gotten a glimpse of him. I knew I was probably just imagining what I wanted to imagine.

One of the reasons I was willing to take on Jennie as an apprentice was because I knew I couldn't do this by myself. Deep inside me, I felt like I had to finish my current project and then to give it to him. It was as if my soul couldn't find peace until I saw that particular sculpture in his hands.

I hadn't felt so unsettled since I was a child, locked in a schoolroom when my body craved the forest. The mystery man had saved my life, and that was how I justified the obsession, but deep down, I knew it was more than that, something primal. Even as I lay in excruciating pain in the Emergency Department, I knew I needed to lay eyes on him and couldn't go into surgery until I saw his face.

Damn, the Goddess. I knew she was behind it. I'd felt it as I looked up at her after the log rolled across my leg. Speaking of that bitch of a log, it deserved to be stripped, split, and sawed into pieces. A perfect project for Jennie's first turn at the sawmill.

I told Jennie what I wanted each log to be cut into, and even though I only lasted until lunchtime before I was driven back to the house for another pain pill, she and Lee continued working. Jennie might've technically been my apprentice, but she couldn't have a better person than Lee working with her on the basics.

Lee had taught me everything I needed to know about forestry. My father had covered basic tree cutting, and even taught me the farm trade, but it wasn't my forte, and to his credit, he recognized that early enough. He and Lee had been close, and when I showed interest in learning the forestry trade, he sent me to train with Lee and Indigo.

I knew Lee was disappointed that his daughter and I hadn't clicked. She and I had seen each other over the years, but by the time I was doing my internship with

Lee, she was doing hers with a coven in Chemeketa, or Che, the name most people used for the pagan community on the coast.

Back at the house, I took my pill and rested my leg before drifting to sleep.

I was back on the hill, but instead of fog, there was sunshine. I saw Creagan, but there was a film between us. I tried to move toward him, but once again, my feet were trees grown into the hillside.

He turned toward me, his eyes as green as the forest and his face sad. I yelled for him, but he didn't seem to be able to hear me. I willed the earth to let me go, and as I struggled, I was able to pull loose from the ground and move toward him. But my legs weren't legs, they were still roots, and I stumbled and fell before rolling down the hill away from where he stood motionless, watching me.

When I woke, I was covered in sweat, and my leg throbbed. I could tell I'd been twisting and turning in my sleep.

I got up and stumbled into the kitchen, seeing Indigo there. "Hi, Indigo," I said, and she turned to look at me.

Her eyes glowed, and I could see the prophecy in them. Indigo was what we called a hedge witch. She had always been sought out, especially when things needed clarity that involved access to the other side.

"You are in danger, Eli. Your destiny brings you directly in the line of fire. Be warned, you must be strong and follow your instincts, or your life could be in peril." The strange glow began to dim, and as she turned away, she whispered, *"You will only win through love."*

Indigo lost her balance then, and I had to rush forward to keep her from falling.

"What did I say?" she asked.

"You gave me a warning," I said. "You said my life was in danger, and love was how I'd win."

She nodded. "I don't do too well with these visions any longer. It sucks to get older, lad." She patted my cheeks, then looked at my flushed skin.

"You've been having your own visions, I can see. The smell of them is still on you."

I shrugged. "Just a dream."

The older woman chuckled. "If only. I've always thought life might be easier if we could just toss our dreams and visions aside like the rest of the population, but it isn't quite as easy for us now, is it?"

I shook my head. "No, it isn't."

She patted my hand. "You should go see Meredith. She's much better at prophecy than I am these days."

I laughed out loud. "No, thank you," I said, causing Indigo to laugh. Meredith had decided I was more bisexual than homosexual and had made it her mission to seduce me. I'd had to have a very serious talk with her over the last solstice celebration about boundaries.

She had been more than a little drunk and threatened to turn me into a warthog. I had to remind her of the three times rule and the fact that the Fae blood ran just as thick in me as it did in her. She stomped off, cursing me, and three days later, I got a huge wart next to my nose.

The next time I saw Lee after that, he chuckled while telling me Meredith had broken out in the worst rash he'd ever seen, and was having to have massive doses of steroids to keep the outbreak from seriously damaging her skin.

I rubbed my wart and said to Lee, "It isn't like I didn't remind her."

The wart finally disappeared, and I assumed Meredith's face had returned to normal. Still, I was in no mood to see her again anytime soon.

I didn't need to have my dreams interpreted. I'd been put on a path that involved me and the man who'd found me. The dreams, Indigo's warning, all of it pointed toward that, toward him.

I figured the best thing I could do was to finish my sculpture and give it to him. Maybe these weird dreams would stop then. Maybe, if I was lucky, that was all the Goddess required of me.

Chapter Eight

Crea

I KNEW I HAD to go back to Chemeketa the day I'd woken up after my dream. Grandma's place that sat overlooking the ocean, with its gentle stream that flowed past the house and down a deep ravine into the Pacific, was picturesque.

I knocked on the door of my grandmother's old house and her roommate, Drew, answered, smiling. "Hey, Crea," he said. "I'm glad you were able to come. Gwen wanted you to have the things she left you."

I came in and shook the man's hand. We chatted a few minutes before he took me upstairs. I'd told him on the phone I'd had a dream about her, and how she'd said I needed to pick up something she'd left me. When he confirmed as much, I immediately caught a flight to Oregon.

Three large chests sat in the center of the room. When I opened the one Drew said was mine, it was full of stuff I'd had when I was a kid. Mostly it held only sentimental value, but it made me happy to go through my childhood treasures. I had to admit, though, nothing spoke to me as the reason I'd needed to come this far.

When I walked down out of the attic, Drew was waiting for me. He handed me a small box, and said, "Gwen told me to give this to you. That it'd be something you needed."

I took the curious wooden box that was adorned with strange carvings of trees and rocks that seemed to be intertwined. When I opened it, I recognized the emerald right away. "Cool," I said, and Drew chuckled.

"That was part of your grandmother's wedding ring. I helped her find an artist to make this for you."

"It's beautiful, but her ring was made with yellow gold. Is this silver?"

"No, it's titanium. She said you needed something stronger than gold to survive what you were up against."

"Did Grandma tell you about the curse?" I asked.

He shook his head. "No, she wasn't one to share other people's personal information, but if there's a curse on you, she would've been determined to undo it. I'm willing to go out on a limb here and say this is part of that undoing process."

I shrugged. "Maybe, but don't hold your breath. I have a tendency to only attract the wackos."

"Don't feel bad," he said. "As a fellow gay man, I can tell you, one doesn't have to be cursed to have that skill."

I knew from meeting Drew when Grandma still lived here that he was gay. Unfortunately for me, I didn't feel anything sexual toward him *at all*. He was attractive, smart, funny, loved our grandma, but he was not for me, and that was crystal clear from the moment we'd first met.

Drew helped me bring the chest down, so I could send it home. I stuck the wooden box in my pocket, wishing

I knew where it'd come from. When I asked Drew, he just shrugged. "She's had it since I've been around. It used to sit on a shelf with three others that now have matching things for your brothers. Your brothers will get the others when they visit, which was her requirement, of course."

"That's strange. I only have two brothers. Is the other one for Jennie, my niece?"

He shrugged. "I honestly don't know. There's a note attached to each box that I'm supposed to open when one of you calls. That's where my instructions end. It's all very cloak and dagger."

"Sounds like her." I smiled, feeling nostalgic. "I sure do miss her."

"Yeah, me too. Well, sort of. She hasn't really gone away yet."

"Really, you think she's haunting you?"

"No, I wouldn't call it a haunting, more like hanging out, but don't be concerned. Your grandma was never one to be confined by conventions. She'll go when she's ready."

I couldn't help but chuckle. He knew her well.

I slipped the ring on my finger. "I like that she made this for me, it makes me feel closer to her. If you don't mind, let me know who number four is. I can't wait to see what she did with the other stones. Grandma's ring was weird, but pretty, and this one is amazing."

"I'll do that, but let's keep these a secret for now. Your brothers need to come to get theirs when it's their time to do so. I think she's enjoying the process of bringing you all back home. That's my gut feeling anyway."

"I think you're right. Besides, the dream I had was strange and vivid, although I can't remember much about it. Just that my dad was there in all his hateful splendor, and she wanted me to come get the ring, although I had no idea at the time it was a ring."

I hugged Drew again, wishing there was some kind of sexual energy between us, but feeling nothing but the affection I'd have for anyone who'd loved my grandmother the way he had. I took my leave for the airport, stopping at the UPS Store on the way to ship the chest back home.

I thumbed over the little box on the flight back to San Francisco. The work was delicate and fine. I guessed it was possible Grandma had done it herself, but the level of intricate detail suggested someone else who had massive artistic talent. I looked on the bottom and around the inside for a name, but there was no clue as to who'd made it.

The emerald was huge. It sparkled like a star, but the color was rich and dark. I'd always had a thing for emeralds, and I suspected it was because of this one in particular.

When I was little, my grandma said I was the emerald, that I'd come from the earth and was her representative. Being an earth spirit herself, she'd told me I would always do well with growing things, building things with wood and stone.

In fact, my name, Creagan, is an old Gaelic word for rocks. My mom, who hated everything about my grandmother and her mystical ways, had been the one to name me. The story she told was she'd heard the name while she and Dad were hiking in Scotland. She'd found out she was pregnant while they were on the trip, and had decided if she had a boy, that'd be my name.

So, it made sense I was an earth energy. At least it made sense in the world that was my grandma's.

I put the ring back on as the plane descended. The second it touched the skin, I felt a little pang and thought of the lumberjack I'd saved while driving up to Crater Lake. *Strange*, I thought, but when it came to my grandma, what wasn't?

Chapter Nine

Eli

JENNIE WAS PERFECT. LIKE she's been sent from the Goddess, which I didn't doubt. Not only was she smart, funny, and kept me in good spirits, she also loved the wood and seemed to have a natural, almost innate skill with it.

I recognized so much of myself in her, but thinking of the kid who told me in his application that he was a younger version of me, I kept that thought to myself.

With Lee's help, Jennie quickly learned the sawmill, and within a week, all the logs were cut and placed in my vacuum kiln to dry. I'd splurged on the fancy kiln a few years back to celebrate my artistic success, but even with the reduced time, it still took a couple weeks for the sawn lumber to dry to the point where I could work with it.

I used that time to show Jennie some of the carving techniques along with which tools did what. She listened with rapt attention. When I asked her to show me what she'd used for the little raccoon, she blushed and pulled a little pocket knife out of her pocket.

I laughed, which caused her blush to deepen. "No worries, my first tools were my mom's kitchen knives and a couple of screwdrivers I sharpened, but once you use these, you'll never go back to the pocketknife."

She took to the carving tools like a fish to water. Because we had plenty of time to waste until the lumber was dry, I let her experiment with each one, helping her perfect her technique. By the time the lumber was ready, I'd swear I had enough sawdust stuck in my cast to build a new tree. It was itching like a son of a bitch. I'd pulled out my wall calendar a week after Jennie arrived and started marking off the days until the damned cast could be taken off. Two weeks, that was all I had to wait. It amazed me how much time had passed since the accident and hiring my apprentice. Sometimes big things happened in life, and it felt like it'd always been that way. That was how it felt having Jennie around. Her love of discovery reignited my passion, and I was chomping at the bit to get the project done.

When we pulled the boards out of the kiln, Jennie was like a little kid on Christmas morning. Her eyes were wide with excitement, especially as she reexamined the gnarled pieces. The woman was made for this. Now that she was working with me, I questioned why it'd taken me so long to take on an apprentice.

My stamina improved daily, and under normal circumstances, I'd have been happy to dig into the wood the evening we pulled it out, but my instincts told me I should go home and leave Jennie with the pieces to get to know them again before we got started.

So, I left and headed to Lee's. I'd decided when the wood was done, I'd be moving back to my place. Tonight would be my last night staying here, and I wanted to spend it with Lee and Indigo in a way that showed how much I appreciated what they'd done to help me through my injury.

When I got to the house, Indigo met me at the door, concern clouding her face.

"Indigo, what's wrong? Is Lee okay?" I asked.

"Yes, he's fine. Eli, Miranda came to visit me this morning. She had a vision that concerns you, and I need you to hear it from her."

I gulped. "Miranda's here?" I asked.

"Yes," I heard a voice say from behind Indigo. "But don't worry, I've not been drinking, *and* I've sworn off curses for the rest of my life."

"Hi, Miranda," I said, doing everything in my power not to shudder.

She laughed. "I totally deserve your reaction. If it helps, I felt bad immediately after I cursed you, but was too drunk to undo it. I'm sure you know I paid a high price for it."

I nodded, but didn't dare speak.

"Anyway, I'll deliver my message and be on my way. Can we sit down? It's not always easy dealing with the spirit realm, especially regarding important stuff."

Indigo led us into her living room, and we sat across from each other.

Miranda began by saying, "Indigo told me you've been having dreams and that she'd had a prophetic message. She also asked me to look into it deeper than she felt comfortable doing. When I did, I was immediately struck with a vision, one that almost caused me to black out." Miranda scooted up in her seat and pinned me with her eyes. "Eli, I'm a trained hedge witch, Indigo was my mentor, and she sent me to work with some of the most powerful hedge witches in the country. I've never had anything this intense come at me before. You need to understand this, because it very well could mean the difference between life and death for you."

I leaned back, unsure what to say or do, so I just remained quiet.

Miranda looked at Indigo, then leaned back herself, drew in a deep breath and let it out. She closed her eyes for a few moments like I'd seen Indigo do when she was about to do a reading, then when she opened them, the strange glow that accompanied hedge witches when they prophesied came over her.

"You are about to begin working on a project again. One you've already started, but in your mind's eye, you see changes in the piece. These changes are because you've met someone, an important someone who has the power to change your destiny forever. Be warned, Eli, these changes are themselves a spell, an undoing of an evil act between father and son. Undoing a spell like that is powerful magic. As with the curse I cast against you, once done, it can't be undone. The consequences of it must be felt and the process honored until it comes to its conclusion. Sometimes, a curse is too powerful to reach its own conclusion, and must be undone through other means, but those who dare to take on a curse must face a difficult and wily foe. As with any magic, you have the choice to accept it or not, but you need to know, you will be accepting it if you finish this project."

Miranda closed her eyes and shook off the spell she was under. When she opened them, she looked drained.

Indigo crossed to her and laid her hand on her crown chakra. *"This is my choice, so let it flow, energy cross through me and into your soul. So mote it be."* Indigo chanted, and from under her hand a hazy purple halo glowed.

When the light dimmed, Miranda looked as if she'd just taken a dose of caffeine.

She patted Indigo's hand and thanked her.

"Eli, do you understand the warning?" she asked.

I nodded. My stomach was in knots, and I wasn't sure I could respond without squeaking.

"Good," she said, and stood to go. "If you have questions, ask me or Indigo, but you must be absolutely sure you want to take this on before you go into your workshop tomorrow. If you touch that piece, I'm afraid things will change for you and never be the same again."

I nodded and managed to thank her.

When she'd left with Indigo, I went to my bedroom and lay down. "Goddess, give me insight," I prayed, and closed my eyes.

I stood on the beach in Chemeketa, looking out over the ocean, the giant old-growth trees behind me. I heard him approach, and when I turned, he was completely naked with the moon's rays cloaking him.

He was utterly beautiful with those emerald eyes and slight body. He came toward me as if he'd known me for years. The look in his eyes was that of a lover, playful and eager. When his lips touched mine, I pulled him into an embrace, and for the first time, I knew what it felt like to be home.

The vision changed almost instantly, and I stood back in the clear-cut forest, but where the chainsaws had cut the trees, blood seemed to be flowing from the stumps. The black fog seemed to be feeding off the blood, evil and something that felt just wrong—hatred and raw negativity.

I saw the man I'd been holding seconds earlier, but he was old now. He was drawn and empty, his hair white and listless. All the energy that had been inside him when I held him mere seconds earlier was gone. I walked toward him, concerned. As I reached him, he was no longer there. Instead, he had transformed into one of the trunks, and the blood flowing out of him was real. The fog wasn't drinking the blood of a real tree, it was feeding off his blood.

The little woman in tie-dye stood next to me then and sighed. When I looked at her, she was crying. "This is what has been done to him. If someone isn't able to free him from the curse that feeds off his strength..."

She turned to me and wiped her eyes. "Will you be his champion?" she asked.

I didn't know how to answer. "I don't know him," I replied.

"In your soul you do, look deeper," she commanded.

I looked back over the stump of a person in front of me, and an overwhelming feeling of protection came over me. I wanted to save him, just like I wanted to save the trees but had never had the power to.

"Will you be his champion?" she asked again.

This time I just said, "I don't know."

She looked down and sighed. "If not, then this is his destiny."

I opened my eyes, and I was lying on the bed. I felt a bit of the tiredness Miranda must have felt.

I got up to go into the living room and realized the sun was coming up. *What time is it?* I wondered, and when I saw my clock, it read six thirty in the morning. I'd slept the entire evening and morning away.

When I came out of my room, both Lee and Indigo were sitting across from each other. They both had their eyes closed and appeared to be in a trance. I crossed to them and sat on the stool. They both lifted their heads simultaneously and looked at me, exhaustion clearly present on both their faces.

"You're done then?" Lee asked.

I nodded. "Did you do this?" I asked them.

"No," Indigo said, shaking her head. "But we assumed it was going to happen. We just made the path clearer for you."

I sighed. "Thanks, I have a clear vision of what decision I need to make."

"And what will that be?" Lee asked.

"I'm going to rescue him," I said, matter of fact.

I knew neither of them knew who the *him* I was referring to was, but as I'd watched him bleeding out on that hillside, I knew it had always been my destiny to save him. It was our destiny to save each other. I guessed from how powerful it felt to be with him that it had always been our destiny. Miranda had gotten that wrong. This wasn't a change in destiny, it was my acceptance of it.

When I got to the workshop, Jennie was sitting on a chair I had out front. "Hey," I said, and when she looked up at me, she looked tired. "Couldn't sleep?"

"No, I slept, but it wasn't pleasant."

I instantly felt guilty. I hadn't thought what I was going through would affect my apprentice, which was stupid since she was connected to me now. Of course, it would affect her.

"Tell me about it," I said, and pulled an old bucket over to sit beside her.

"I had nightmares about my family, my uncles and great-grandma, and even some shadow figure who was chasing us."

I nodded. "Yeah, that's the same as me. I'm afraid we have some strange magic about. How much do you know about Chemeketa?" I asked her.

"Well, I know it's full of witches and people who still practice paganism. My great-grandma was a convert to Wicca, that's why she settled there."

"Well, apparently, the piece we're working on is linked to some of that power, and to my destiny in particular. I'm afraid you being my apprentice has pulled you into something none of us expected."

She nodded. "Well, I guess it is what it is, but dang, those dreams were scary. Almost real."

I put my hand on hers and said, "I totally get it. It was a rough night for me too. So, here's the deal." I decided to come clean about it all. I shouldn't be making choices that impacted her. She needed to make her own choices. "This project, the one we're starting today, that's the issue. Once I start on it, the die is cast, so to speak. If you want to avoid the drama and possible danger associated with it, you probably need to break our agreement, otherwise I can't guarantee you won't be pulled into it."

She sat for a moment and sighed. "This has something to do with me and my family as well. I'm not sure how, but it does. I'm not leaving. This feels important, almost like it's my destiny too."

"In that case, are you ready to get started?"

She looked at me, and I could see the fire in her eyes. "Damned straight," she said, then laughed. "Unless you're gay, then, gayly forward!"

I laughed out loud at her comment. "I'm not," I said.

She shrugged. "It's okay. I figured you were probably straight."

I laughed again. "No, I'm not straight. I'm gay as can be, so"–I stood up and held out my hand to help her up–"let's move gayly forward!"

I wasn't sure what I expected, maybe sparks flying off the wood, or some sort of magic flowing around, but there was nothing spectacular to indicate we were working on a magical piece, or that my destiny was involved. Rather, it just felt right and easy to put energy into, and it felt even more right, if that was possible, that I was doing it with an apprentice.

I cut the lumber the size I wanted, then using the natural resins I preferred over synthetic glues, I combined the different pieces of wood. In my mind's eye, I imagined how each different shade of wood would accent the piece. This was an abstract sculpture, but it represented the love of the forest, the respect for the land, and hopefully would inspire conservation for the old-growth forests we still had left. When I was done, the piece would be one foot by two feet. I wanted it to be substantial, but not overwhelming.

When my leg started cramping, I went over to the chair I kept near the workbench and watched Jennie as she progressed with the pieces I wanted her to sand down on the turntable. Wood that would line the inner aspects of the sculpture. I was pleased to see she'd gone into what I call a creative trance. That was good. It indicated the young woman was able to feel the wood and let her creative mind take over. That was a skill I couldn't teach her. It had to be innate.

When she finished the detailed piece, she pulled it off and showed it to me. I let it flow into my hand and said, "Close, real close," then showed her the places where the sanding needed to remove more of the wood. I didn't know if she was aware I'd thrown her into the deep end of the pool. Figuring out how to sand a piece so it met the vision I had in my mind was difficult enough for me. Jennie was a beginner, and even though I'd described my vision, unless there was a connection, I knew she'd never be able to recreate it.

I guess I wanted to see her natural talents, along with her ability to connect with me. Both pleased me. She spun the wood and sanded it to where I wanted and had almost made it look exactly as I'd seen in my head.

That was good because, to be honest, with the screaming in my leg after only a couple of hours, I doubted I could work on the finer details.

Jennie ended up sanding off too much, and I could see the frustration on her face. "I made several starts, just in case. I figured you'd mess a couple up. Don't beat yourself up, though, practice makes perfect."

She seemed to take the mistake in stride, and when she went at the second one, I could tell she'd learned from it. About an hour later, she handed me the piece, and I smiled. "Perfect, Jennie. It's absolutely perfect. Now, make ten more of them." I expected her to complain. I figured I would've complained, but instead, she smiled, took another blank and began the next one.

About halfway through the afternoon, I decided I'd had enough and took the ATV back to Lee's. I'd fully intended to move back to my place, which was only down the road from my workshop, and butted up against Lee's place. Unfortunately, I had a wood stove and knew I didn't have enough to keep a fire going all night, and besides, my leg was beginning to hurt again. I'm glad I didn't tell them I was moving out because right now, I really just wanted to lie back down.

When I got to the house and walked into the kitchen, I saw Indigo standing over her little work area in the breakfast nook. She was working on something woven, although I wasn't sure what, from where she was standing.

"Do you have any coffee left from this morning?" I asked.

She looked over at me and shook her head. "No, and from the look of you, you need less coffee and more sleep. Sit down, and I'll get you a glass of milk. I'm working on something to keep the dreams at bay. Unfortunately, when you have a prophetic project in the works, the dreams can become... well, they can become unrelenting." She chuckled. "Sometimes, you need something that works as a filter, keeping the same dream from harassing you, but still allowing you to see what you need when you need it."

I sighed. "Indigo, that sounds good. I was dreading sleep, not sure I could handle seeing the visions from last night again."

She put a glass of milk down in front of me and smiled. "Sometimes, it's difficult to manage the gifts we've been given. The fairy sight can weigh heavily on the human mind. You'll need to learn to control it and allow your humanity to rest. That's something we teach our hedge witches early on. Our community needs to do a better job teaching these controls to everyone." She turned back to her work.

"We are all spread out these days. It's not like it was back in the early days of Chemeketa. Now we just have our summer solstice week and the camp. I think I'm going to start teaching a class about protection and managing the gifts," she continued, after a pause. "I guess seeing what you've been dealing with these past few days has shown me how much that's needed, and although I don't do the scrying like I used to, I certainly still have the skills necessary for helping you younger folks manage what you've got."

I smiled and would've gotten up to give her a hug if my leg wasn't pounding like it was.

She looked over at me and frowned. "Your leg's hurting you, isn't it?"

I nodded.

"Well, finish that milk and then go to bed. I'll hang this little basket over your bed when I'm done."

I smiled. "You are a credit to our craft," I told her, and she smiled.

"I'm an old woman who's lucky to still have any gift left, but thank you, sweet boy," she replied.

When I reached my room, I could smell the smudge Indigo had clearly done. I also saw a few twigs of lavender attached to the headboard, and I smiled. The woman had probably been working on this room since I'd left.

I fell asleep the moment I closed my eyes and when I found myself standing in the field, I moaned.

"Oh, stop being a big baby," the strange tie-dye-clad lady said with humor as she came around to stand in front of me.

"Who are you?" I asked.

"Just an old woman," she replied. "So, I see you've got a little help filtering these visions. That's good. You'll need all the help you can get."

"I don't understand what this is all about," I told her, and waited for her response.

"It'll all become clearer as you go along, just trust the Goddess to guide you. I can hold him off for a little while longer, at least long enough for you to get to know each other, but eventually, you and he must take this on. He grows stronger while I grow weaker, so eventually, I won't be able to hold him back."

"Who is he, and what is all this about?" I asked.

"I wish I could tell you, but it's not for me to do so. That is someone else's responsibility," she replied, and the image of the man who'd saved me rose in front of us.

"Trust your feelings for him, trust him even though he won't trust you. He's going to be too afraid of you."

I shook my head. "Why won't he trust me?" I asked, and she looked sad.

"He's been cursed by someone who should've loved him. The betrayal isn't something easily overcome, but

overcome he must if he's going to fight off the darkness that wants to engulf him."

"I'll try, but I don't know how I can help."

I looked over to where the old woman had stood, but she was gone.

I must have slept okay after that because I didn't remember anything until I woke up a few hours later. When I opened my eyes, there was the woven pouch I'd seen Indigo working on earlier. I had to wonder if that was what caused the dream to end and for me to sleep. If so, I was thankful. The old woman who kept coming to my dreams was a harmless creature, but I needed sleep more than I needed to chat. Although I was getting an idea of what was headed my way. I just hoped I was indeed strong enough to help the man overcome the darkness that plagued him.

Jennie and I worked on the project every day over the next few weeks. By the time I had my cast removed, it was almost finished.

Having my leg freed from that blasted cast felt like magic. They gave me a removable cast to replace it, but damn, it felt good to scratch the itchy places that had been out of reach so long. When the sawdust fell out, the doctor gave me a look, and I shrugged. "A man's gotta work for a living," I said, but she wasn't amused.

With the cast gone, I was able to help Jennie do the intricate, detailed work, and before I knew it, the project was done.

Both Jennie and I sat back and admired the work. "It's beautiful," she said. "I can't believe I was part of helping you do that."

I smiled. "It still amazes me when a project is done too. It's like the work already exists, and all I do is follow the directions to help it manifest itself."

"That's exactly how this feels," Jennie said, and grabbed me into a hug.

I chuckled. I'd grown very attached to the young woman over the past few weeks. She'd stopped just being my apprentice and had become a part of my family. Even Lee and Indigo seemed to feel the same way, and we were all enjoying our evenings together.

"So, now what?" Jennie asked as we both stared at the piece again.

"We deliver it," I said, and the words caused my heart to leap in my chest. I took a deep breath and let it out slowly.

Jennie looked at me and frowned. "That scary, huh?"

I nodded. "It's something... not sure how I feel yet, but it's something. Help me pack it up, and we'll clean the workshop and put all the tools away. We can head to San Francisco tomorrow."

"Really, San Francisco?" she asked. "My uncle lives there. Want me to see if he'll let us stay with him?"

I laughed. "No, I'd prefer to stay in a hotel. I'm not sure what all this will involve. It could be smooth with no problems, or it could turn upside down when he sees it." She nodded, but looked confused. "I'll explain later," I said, trying to avoid getting into the fact that we'd be showing up unannounced to see a guy I'd met once and then only briefly. "But, for now, we seriously need to pack this and get it into my Jeep."

Now that the cast was off, I felt a hundred percent better. Not totally healed by any means, but at least I didn't have to take naps in the middle of the day. I also slept like a baby. With Indigo's sleep pouch hanging over my bed, I hadn't had any more dreams or visits from the crazy lady in the tie-dye. Rather, I slept like a log and woke up feeling refreshed and ready for the next day.

That was often how things felt when I was working on a project, and the fact that Jennie and I were so perfectly in step, made things exciting and fun. I'd discovered I really enjoyed showing her things and watching her learn and grow. I couldn't help but think if I'd ever had a kid, this was what it would have felt like to show them how to use the workshop and equipment.

When the workshop was back in order, I went to my office and pulled out one of the sparkling wines my cousin had begun specializing in after he took over the family vineyard. I found some Brie and Tillamook cheese I'd sliced a couple days before, anticipating the end of the project, and went out to where Jennie was finishing up the last of the sweeping.

I put the cheese on the flat top of the table saw, went back to the office to pull out two cups I kept there for coffee, and brought those out as well. Jennie had already dug into the cheese, and I realized we hadn't broken for lunch today. She was probably starving.

"This will likely go to our heads on an empty stomach, but, oh well, it can't be helped. We need to celebrate." I pulled the cork as I spoke.

When it made a satisfying popping sound, Jennie cheered. I poured two good measures into our cups, picked up some of the sharp cheddar, and ate at least one slice before I took a drink.

I lifted the cup, and said, "To the first project of many!"

Jennie tapped her cup to mine, saying, "Hear, hear," and we drank. "Mmm, that's yummy," she said.

"It is," I replied, and let the flavors of the sparkling Pinot Noir spread over my tongue. "It was grown and made on the vineyard where I grew up. My cousin runs it now, and he started using my dad's old grapes to make this. I like it more than the regular wine we used to make."

"My dad would love this. He's really a big Champagne lover."

I smiled. "I spoke to him, you know. He seemed like a nice guy."

"He is most of the time. Strict though."

I laughed. "You should've spent some time with mine. He was an old farmer all his life and believed in strict discipline."

"Mine just had big plans for me. They really didn't work out too well, though. I feel like I've disappointed him."

"I think you can let that go. From what he told me that day, he was just happy you were finding your footing."

She nodded, but kept a frown on her face. "I think it's hard for my parents. My mom is, as you know, a famous writer, my dad is a successful model who landed several big modeling gigs before anyone found out he was trans."

The lights came on for me then, and I shook my head. "I'd forgotten your mom was married to Russ Elliott. Your dad is way cool. I actually met him at the New York gala when I delivered the piece I made for the Metropolitan Museum."

"He is cool. I love him, and Mom and my sperm daddy too, but they are all so high energy!"

I laughed and almost spat out the wine. "Sperm daddy?"

She smiled. "Yeah, my parents' friend, who's become a high-powered attorney, was their sperm donor. I don't think they expected him to be a part of my life like he is, but I sort of demanded it from an early age. I never knew what to call him, though. I had a father, and sperm donor seemed sort of gross even when I was little, so I called him my sperm daddy. He grew up here in Chemeketa and brought me out to visit his grandmother while she was still alive. That's actually how I ended up here."

We toasted her family, and as I suspected, the wine went right to my head. We finished off the cheese and sat around the rest of the afternoon chatting about family. We talked a little about Chemeketa, and I found out she'd never been to the big summer festivals there.

"You aren't pagan then?" I asked.

She shook her head. "No, I'm not really anything. My sperm daddy wasn't really involved with Chemeketa, and I didn't see my great-grandma that much, mostly because she was so far away, and well, I had my other grandparents, so it wasn't until after I graduated that I decided to spend time there and get to know the place."

I sighed. "It's really an amazing place, but you need to go to the festival. It'll be interesting, and you have friends there now too. Didn't you mention that when we first met?"

I noticed a blush for the first time, and knew then there was more to that story than what she'd told me.

"I don't know. I only met her when I visited my great-grandmother, she was her neighbor. When my great-grandmother died, I decided to come out and spend time at her house, but her roommate was away on vacation or something. Scarlett was in charge of watching the house for him, and she found me sitting on the garden bench. I was feeling really out of sorts when she found me. I'd always felt like I'd missed out on something by not knowing my sperm daddy's family better. Like there was something there, something important I'd missed. Scarlett felt sorry for me and invited me to stay at her parents' house."

"If your grandmother was a natural witch, you do have her heritage. What we call a birthright."

"Yeah, that's what Scarlett said. She tried to show me basic things, but I don't have the skills or the interest. It just made me feel weird when Scarlett or her mom cast spells, like I was imposing on sacred space or something."

I smiled at her. "I doubt you were imposing. They wouldn't have let you in if they hadn't trusted you and wanted you there. It's a huge honor to be asked to join in someone's circle."

She nodded. "Well, I'm clearly not a witch, although I wish I could be. I feel more drawn to the forests around there, to the trees and to the animals that live in the forests." She lit up as she spoke. "Did you know there are bears and mountain lions all around there? I saw them both while I was visiting Scarlett's family. A mountain lion came within a few feet of me, and I should've been afraid she was going to attack me, but..." She hesitated as she worked to find the words. "...I could tell she didn't mean me any harm. It's almost like she was laughing at me."

I smiled. "I've seen them in the wild there too, but don't be too confident around them. Cougars are still big cats, and can change their mind about attacking within moments. Anytime they're around, you should try to make yourself look bigger, to encourage them to leave you alone."

She nodded, but I could tell she wasn't convinced she was in danger.

"The day before I crushed my leg, I saw a mother bear and three baby cubs who were just coming out of hibernation. If I hadn't been on my ATV, I'd have been concerned. You could feel the hunger coming off them."

"Yeah, that's what I thought about the bear I saw too. It was a big male, but he was too far away to be any danger."

"Don't assume that," I warned her. "Bears can move a lot faster than you think they can. This isn't New York. Our wildlife here can be seriously dangerous."

She smiled and nodded. "Is this you playing the protective parent?" she asked, teasing me.

"Maybe. Got to protect my apprentice. Could you imagine all the work it would take to train someone new now that I've just got you up to speed?"

She smiled and tapped me with her elbow affectionately.

The wine had finally worn off, so I went back, grabbed another bottle, and Jennie and I headed over to Lee and Indigo's to celebrate with them.

I'd moved back into my place the week before, but had already told Lee I thought we'd be done before the evening was out, and Indigo said she wanted to fix us a celebratory dinner. I had a feeling Indigo would miss the chance to mother me after I left.

On the way over, a large black raven flew over us and stopped on the path. At first, I figured it was just a normal raven, and I drove toward him, thinking he'd move as we got closer. Instead, the bird turned toward us, and when we approached, he jumped up and landed on the front of the vehicle.

Both Jennie and I stared at the bird, not knowing what to think. After a moment, the bird, staring us in the eye, flew up and settled in one of the trees above us.

It followed us all the way to Lee and Indigo's, staying just a few feet away. When we got to the house, Indigo was waiting for us on her front stoop, holding a plate of what looked like corn kernels. "Come stand behind me," she said, looking up at the bird. When we complied, she walked over to the tree where the raven sat, still watching us closely. "We bring this treat to you, our brother."

The raven swooped down and acted like he was going to land on Indigo's head. She didn't move or flinch, just stood until the raven landed in the tree again. When he did, she bent down and poured the corn on the ground.

"You are welcome here, brother, until you have finished your meal, but then you must go."

The bird regarded her, made a sound like he was laughing, but didn't attempt to fly down again.

Indigo turned and walked toward the front stoop and motioned us to go in.

"What was that about?" I asked the moment we were inside.

Indigo shook her head. "Let's eat while he does," she said. "We'll see what he does after that."

I opened the wine and poured us all a glass while Lee and Indigo put the food out. We were all silent after the raven incident.

"So, you are done then," Indigo said loud enough that the raven could hear through the open window.

Immediately the bird started croaking loudly, and within seconds, he was joined by several others.

When I almost said something, Indigo put her hand up to silence me, and we sat in silence for several moments, listening to the birds as they flew around the house.

When the croaking stopped, Indigo stood up and went to the door. She opened it, looked outside, then turned toward me.

Without speaking, she motioned me over, and when I came up behind her, she pointed to where the corn had been. I could see a large feather there, one from the bird's wings.

"That's for you," she said. "But know before you accept it, Raven is a trickster and has the ability to shape shift. They rarely give a gift to humans, preferring to take from us, but this must be important. Ravens are also messengers from the other worlds, so the feather can be a true gift indeed if you find you need assistance speaking with those who've gone before us."

I immediately thought of the funny old lady from my dreams and walked toward the feather, reached down, and picked it up.

As soon as I stood up, I saw the woman standing in front of me. She winked, then disappeared.

When I came back to the house, Jennie was staring out toward where I'd just come from. She had gone pale, and I asked her if she was okay.

"Did you see her? The old woman?" she asked.

I nodded. "Yeah, she's visited me several times in dreams. This is the first time I've seen her while awake though."

"That's my great-grandma," Jennie said.

That was a shock, but it also strangely made sense. Jennie had figured out early on she was somehow involved with this. Now we had confirmation. "It'll be okay, she's been my guide through all this. Maybe she pulled you into it for a reason."

Jennie just nodded, continuing to look toward the area where her great-grandmother had briefly appeared.

As we finished eating, Jennie was very quiet. I'd put the feather next to me on the table, and Jennie kept looking at it. Finally, I asked, "Do you want to hold it?"

She shook her head. "No, I'm still too freaked out."

I chuckled. "Welcome to our world."

She looked at me, bewildered. "Does this happen often? People's dead grandparents show up out of nowhere?"

Indigo laughed this time. "Not often, but it isn't that unusual either."

Between bites, Indigo explained, "Ravens are magical creatures both in Europe and America. When Chemeketa was settled, the Native peoples were still here. As they were driven off the land by white settlers, our people embraced them, and over time, we've learned to live in harmony with each other." Jennie nodded, confirming she was still following, "Often the medicine and magic of the two cultures mix, like it did here today. In some ways, the connections between our two cultures make us stronger and in other ways, it can make things confusing."

Indigo stood and refilled everyone's glass, probably to give Jennie time to get her head around the story, before continuing. "Raven is a messenger as well as a trickster. Mostly they're trouble for humans, but when there's something important afoot, they can be very helpful guides. It seems our friend out there was working in his role as messenger between the two worlds and through the veil." Indigo looked at me then. "That feather is a tool you can use to communicate with the dead, but use it wisely. Once it's gone, it's gone, and you won't get another chance."

I glanced at Jennie, who nodded again in understanding. "That's why my dead great-grandma was who I saw."

Indigo put her hand over Jennie's. "She's not dead, sweetheart, just going through her transition. Nothing to be worried about."

The rest of the evening was uneventful. When I took the feather and slipped it into my pocket, I could feel warmth coming off it. We helped Indigo clear the dishes, and I drove Jennie back to the workshop, and waited until she was inside before heading home.

There was a lot going on, and I was ready for bed. The project had been finished to my standards. I was going to deliver it tomorrow, and hopefully, that meant all this would be coming to an end soon enough.

I fell into bed and dreamed of ravens, and old women floating around in tie-dye dresses, all to smells of wine and cheese.

When morning came, I was more than ready to get up and get going.

Jennie met me, excited to get on the road as well. I could tell she'd used my pitiful makeshift shower to clean up and was wearing makeup, and a cute dress I guessed cost more than one of my power tools.

She chatted the whole six-hour drive. I learned more about her than I had the entire time we'd been working together in the shop.

When we reached the outskirts of San Francisco, I pulled over to stretch and get my head on straight before facing the guy haunting my dreams. We had a quick bite to eat at a truck stop, and I asked Jennie if there was anywhere she'd like me to drop her off, like maybe at her uncle's place.

She shook her head, her eyes big. "I want to see this man and maybe meet him."

I nodded. "Well, it could go really bad. I haven't really met him, not in an official way. He doesn't know I'm coming even, and sure doesn't know what I've brought him."

"So, this guy has no idea he's receiving an Eli Bane sculpture?"

I shook my head. "He probably doesn't even know my name."

"Well, that's all very strange, but this whole thing has been, so we might as well keep it that way."

I chuckled. "You're up for being in the middle of his possible strange reaction?"

"Dude," she laughed. "I wouldn't miss it for the fucking world!"

I put his address into my phone and began following the directions. Jennie had fallen quiet then, watching the urban landscape flow by. I could tell she had a lot of questions but was giving me the space I needed, which I deeply appreciated.

When we pulled onto the final street, Jennie looked at me and asked, "Did you change your mind?"

"Hmm? Change my mind about what?"

"About dropping me off. This is my uncle's street," she said.

"It's just coincidence then," I replied. "I'm just following Google to his address. Your uncle must be a neighbor."

I kept driving until I pulled up to a small, yellow bungalow with perfect hedges along the walkway that led up to the home. There were flower beds planted with pansies since it was still early in the season. I imagined there would be pretty flowers that matched the season as the summer progressed. I undid my seat belt and said, "Showtime!" and turned to Jennie, who was staring at me. "What?" I asked, feeling a bit alarmed by her intense expression.

"Why are we parked in front of my uncle's house?" she asked.

I looked at the little yellow house and then back at her. "Your uncle lives here?" I asked.

She nodded slowly and with a hint of suspicion that didn't escape my notice.

I reached into my pocket and pulled out the handwritten note that the guy had left for me at the hospital, and handed it to Jennie.

"Is that your uncle?"

She paled and nodded.

"Well, that makes sense, I guess," I said, taking the paper back from her. "Maybe you can help me pronounce his name then. I was afraid I'd mispronounce it when I met him."

"That's all you've got to say about this?" she replied.

"Well, Jennie, I have a magical feather in my pocket, I've been harassed by some strange dark figure, and I've watched your uncle bleeding out in my dreams since he rescued me from certain death, so I'm not sure what you want me to say."

I realized I'd crossed a line when her eyes opened wider, and she looked like she was going to be sick. "You saw him bleeding out?" she asked.

"No, wait." I sighed. "It wasn't like that. The dark figure looked like he was sucking the life out of him. In the dream, he was a tree stump, so it wasn't like it can be interpreted as literal."

"But, he's in danger?" she asked, her voice taking on a panicked tone.

I shrugged. "You know about as much as I do. Now we know he's your uncle, though, what were your dreams that night?"

She leaned back. "That dark figure you mentioned, he was menacing, swooping around all three of my uncles. My great-grandmother was the only one who could control him, but she was getting weaker the more she tried. Finally, she turned to me and told me I would have to help them when she no longer could."

"See, it all makes sense now. You're part of this, because you are part of them."

"This doesn't bother you?" she asked.

I shook my head. "It's strange and weird, but these things usually are. I've been in this world all my life, I guess I'm just used to it."

"I'm sure as hell not," she replied, but opened her door. "Crea," she said. "He doesn't go by Creagan, just Crea, like Tray."

"Got it. You wanna knock, or should I?"

"I should text him first. He wasn't expecting me until later tonight," she said.

"Suit yourself, but we're here, and this is gonna be easier than I had planned since I didn't know you were related."

She laughed. "That's true. At least this won't be quite as big a shock."

"Yeah, it still will be," I said. "Last time he saw me, I was being wheeled into surgery. I doubt he ever expected to see me again."

She smiled mischievously then, and I felt suspicion seeping into me.

"Did you know he's gay and single too?" she asked, and I understood why I was uncomfortable with that look.

"Don't even think about it. I'm a very happy bachelor. I doubt he'll want to be fixed up with me either after what he had to go through when we met. It was anything but sexy!" I said. "No playing matchmaker, young lady, or I'll have you doing some nasty work when we get back to the workshop!"

She frowned. "You are no fun, Eli, no fun at all!"

CHAPTER TEN

CREA

I'D JUST FINISHED WORKING to help get the gardens west of town ready for spring planting. Unfortunately, the woman who'd written the grant to fund it had moved away after last year's season ended. San Francisco had gotten so bloody expensive, people came and went like flies. I'd had to be up at the crack of dawn on a Saturday morning, which sucked. Still, I'd had several hours to catch up on after my vacation to Crater Lake and then taking a day off to visit Chemeketa to collect my stuff from Grandma's old house.

The second I stepped out of the shower, I felt the ring grow warm. *Strange*, I thought. I'd pretty much worn it twenty-four seven since leaving Drew's place. It was amazing how the house felt more like it belonged to him now than my late grandma. Oh well, that's how she'd have wanted it.

I'd just finished drying off when I heard the doorbell ring. "Fuck," I said, looking down at my naked body. I was expecting a delivery and didn't want to miss it, so I yelled, "Just a minute, I'm getting dressed!" I grabbed some gym shorts I'd thrown into the dirty clothes basket and slipped them on, rushing down the stairs to the front door. When I pulled the door open, there stood my niece.

"Girl, you just about killed me. I thought you were a delivery I was waiting for."

She looked at me and then down at the skimpy shorts, and said, "What kind of delivery were you expecting?"

"Shut up and get in here," I said, pulling her through the door.

I was just about to hug her when the handsome lumberjack who'd plagued my dreams for over a month stepped inside behind her.

I froze, staring at him. Jennie cleared her throat with what sounded like a chuckle.

"Uncle Crea, this the guy I work for, Eli Bane."

I was stuck. I couldn't speak, couldn't even blink. It was like I'd been tossed into a parallel universe.

The man blushed and let his eyes trail down my naked torso to the small shorts and then back up to my face. The look was purely sexual and made goosebumps pop out on my skin. The reaction was not something I wanted to have in front of my one and only niece, so I shook it off, cleared my throat and managed to squeak out, "Welcome."

I excused myself, ran upstairs and changed into real clothes. I felt the darkness seep in around me then, but I ignored it. My father's curse always seemed to be lurking, and with the dreams I'd been having... now having a hunk in my living room. I just waved it off as that.

I started back down the stairs, which gave me a moment to catch my breath and gather my thoughts. How had the guy I saved end up being Jennie's employer? Why was he here? I vaguely remembered scribbling down my name and address at the hospital, but I never expected him to actually contact me. My suspicion ramped up along with the darkness I'd sensed earlier. Could this guy be using my niece to try to get to me? Were we being taken advantage of? I'd watched something like this just the other night on *Cold Case Files*.

By the time I went back downstairs, my niece was rummaging through my refrigerator and had pulled out some cheese and summer sausage I'd cut up for her when she'd texted asking to spend the night.

I was ready to lay into the guy and confront him, but the moment I saw my niece, I knew I couldn't. She looked happier than I'd seen her in a long time. Like she'd found her place.

I looked at the ridiculously beautiful man, this Eli Bane, noticing for the first time he was every bit as old as me, and my dark thoughts fully took over. Was this man also dating Jennie? Fuck, I'd have to walk a fine line here. If he was a crook, though, I'd be able to get my brother involved. The man was like a bloodhound when it came to sniffing out a bad guy. Ever since our father had cursed him, us, Lance had been all about seeking justice. They could've taken the gown off Lady Justice, wrapped it around him, put a blindfold over his eyes, and they'd have had the perfect figurehead.

The thought of my older brother ripping into his daughter's apparent older lover made me smile, which Jennie must have mistaken for me liking the man.

"So, do you remember him from the accident?" she asked.

I nodded. "Yes, it's good to see you're doing better," I replied, giving a nod in his direction.

"Thanks." The man blushed again. He was definitely doing a lot of blushing for a bad guy. I guessed it was part of his plot... look innocent and get people to trust you, then steal their niece's heart and their money.

"How long are you staying, Jennie?" I asked, trying to get the focus off the man. He was too handsome, with too much sexuality pouring off him, and that was making my skin itch. If I wasn't concerned that he was having sex with my niece, I'd think the guy was coming on to me. Hell, maybe he was. Again, this was way too similar to that TV crime show I'd seen.

She looked at the guy and shrugged. "I don't know. Why don't I borrow your car, Eli, and you two can talk? I'll be back in a little while."

I looked at my niece with suspicion and then watched her walk out of the house, leaving me alone with the lumberjack.

When she was gone, he turned to me. "I-I... damn, this is harder than I thought."

It was as if my emotions had been taken over by some-one else and I was having a hard time holding back the rage. Somehow, I managed to keep my cool.

"I wanted to thank you for what you did for me that day, for finding me and saving me."

I nodded, then before I could stop myself, asked, "How long have you been fucking my niece?"

The guy's mouth dropped open. "*Fucking* your niece?" he asked. I didn't respond, just raised an eyebrow in question and waited for him to reply. "I'm not *fucking* anyone, especially not your niece."

I was literally seeing red as I continued, any semblance of control completely gone. "You clearly have some agenda. Showing up here with her out of the blue. Did you tell her not to text me, so it'd be a surprise?" I asked, watching the color drain from his face.

"I didn't know she was your niece until a few minutes ago when we pulled up at your house."

"I don't believe you. I think this is some cheap trick to steal from us or hurt us, or..."

The guy put his hand up to stop me. The color that had drained a moment before had returned in a full blaze of red fury.

"I'm telling you now, I have no intention of stealing from you, or hurting you or your niece in any way. I came to bring you a thank you present, but clearly, this was a mistake."

He turned toward the door. "No, you don't. It's been tough on my niece since she was little, being torn between her family and ours. Trying to figure out where she fits. I'm not going to have you add to that because of whatever agenda you have going on."

He turned back to me. Even in my enraged state, I could see his anger was gone, replaced by hurt and frustration. "Jennie is my apprentice. I owe you for what you did for me. I won't mention that you dislike me or that we've argued, but I will be leaving. Please let her know to call me when she's ready to go home. I'll call an Uber."

Before I could process what was happening, the guy walked out of my home and down the street. With his departure, the rage was quickly dissipating. "That's fucking weird," I said out loud, then closed the front door and locked it.

I'd have to figure out how to work through this with my niece. Maybe she'd see reason once I explained all the details of what had happened. Jennie was nothing if not bright, so she'd be able to catch on without me having to point the finger.

About an hour after she left, I got a knock on the door and opened it to see Jennie's bewildered face. "Why did Eli leave? He just texted me saying he'd checked into his hotel, and that I was to let him know when we were done."

I shrugged, not wanting to have this conversation, not like this and not yet.

I opened the door wider, and she came in. "I'm fixing dinner. Are you hungry?" I asked.

"No, I grabbed something while I was giving you two time."

"Okay, it won't take me a moment," I said.

Jennie sat at my counter and watched me. "Did you kick him out?" she asked directly.

"No, he left on his own."

"Did you say something that caused him to leave?" she asked with accusation in her tone.

I sighed, mostly because I was having a hard time justifying how I'd treated the man while he was here, but I was going to try to help Jennie see my concerns. "Jennie, did you know I found him on the side of the road half dead?"

"Yes."

"Did he tell you I left my name and contact details for him at the hospital's front desk at his request before he went into surgery?" I asked, willing her to begin to put two and two together.

"No, but Eli showed me what you wrote just a moment before we came in."

I looked at her for a moment, wondering what I should say next.

"My turn," she said. "Did he tell you I responded to an ad he'd sent to the Grange meeting house in Chemeketa, or that no one, including my parents, knew I was there?"

She didn't wait for me to answer. "Did you know he's a renowned artist my mom has been harassing to interview for over a year? And that when he found out who I was, he could've tossed me out on my head just for being her daughter, but he gave me a chance instead? Or..." she continued, working herself into a frenzy, "...did you know that he's been plagued with dreams about you, about you being in danger and that he's been warned to avoid you, so his life isn't put in danger?"

"Jennie," I said to stop her. "Listen to yourself. What you're saying is bizarre." I shook my head, no longer really believing this, but I was still trying to justify my actions. "I think this guy might be a shyster."

She looked at me for a long moment, and sighed. "You're an idiot. Come with me."

She walked toward my front door, and I followed her out, unsure what she was up to.

When we got to his car, a new Jeep Cherokee, she opened the back door and reached in, pulling out what looked like a wrapped ball. She handed it to me, and I almost dropped it, the damned thing was so heavy. After slamming the door shut, she helped me carry it into the house.

When we got inside, we placed it on my dining room table and she carefully unwrapped it.

My heart leapt at seeing the sculpture. It was utterly beautiful and intricate, with various pieces of wood tucked into different elements. It was abstract, a mixture of different meanings, but I could make out human-like figures, trees, and flowers. It was something you'd expect to see in a museum.

"Did you make this?" I asked, and turned toward her.

She was on her phone, and a second later, I heard the voice of someone else on the line.

"Hi, Mom. It's Jennie. Yeah, I'm doing really well. Hey, Mom, I'm at Uncle Crea's house... Mom says, 'Hi,' Uncle Crea."

"Hi back," I replied, confused about what was going on.

"Mom, I have a quick question. How much would you estimate an Eli Bane sculpture like the one in the Metropolitan would go for?"

There was silence for a few moments, then I heard a reply, although I couldn't tell what she'd said.

Jennie's face paled, and it took a moment for her to regain her composure. "Would it hurt the value if an apprentice helped him with that?" she asked, and I could tell she was sidetracked.

"Wow, so that doesn't make a difference if it's an Eli Bane?"

Jennie put her phone on speaker.

"Mom, repeat that value amount so Uncle Crea can hear you."

Jennie's mom said a number, and Jennie looked at me, then at the piece.

The amount of money was insane, and I wondered if maybe this was some sort of joke.

"Okay, that's all I need for now, Mom. Thanks."

Her mother interrupted and asked her about working for Eli, which caused Jennie to cringe.

"Sorry, Mom, I can't really get into that. It feels like it would be violating our agreement."

"Okay, I understand and, honey, your dads and I are so proud of you. Tell Uncle Crea to call his brother. I'm sure he'll have a hundred questions about Eli Bane. He's a big fan as well!"

Jennie laughed and assured her that I'd heard what she'd said.

When Jennie hung up, she looked at me, all amusement gone from her face. "He made that for you, and you heard what my mom said it was worth. I'm no art expert, but considering he made it for the man who saved him, all while suffering intense pain caused by his crushed leg, it's going to go up significantly in value!"

Realization was beginning to filter through my brain. I felt the darkness, the unjustified anger, ebbing away. Now, I needed to deal with this before my niece left and never talked to me again.

"Jennie, I don't know what you want me to say. You showed up at my door unannounced with the guy I'd rescued and I thought you two were... well, *involved*. I thought he was trying to take advantage of you and me."

"*Involved?*" she asked, sounding incredulous. "I'm a lesbian, Uncle Crea."

"Oh, well, I didn't get that memo," I said, embarrassed. I had no doubt my crimson cheeks rivaled that of the blushing lumberjack.

"What did you say to him?"

"Basically, what I just said."

"Damn, Uncle Crea. I should've stayed out of this. He was going to come here by himself. He offered to let me stay home, but I wanted to meet his mystery savior. Neither of us knew it was you until we pulled onto your street."

She glanced at the piece and sat down in a huff. "He worked his ass off on that. You have no idea how much pain he was in, but he was determined to finish it and bring it to you. I feel like this went bad because of me. If I hadn't been with him, what would your reaction have been?" she asked.

I looked at her, then over at the sculpture.

"Surprise, I guess. I'd still have been suspicious, but maybe not in the same way."

She messed with her phone, and while staring at me, dialed what I assumed was his number. When I heard a man answer, I was sure it was him.

"Hi, Eli. I'm here with my uncle, and he has something he wants to say to you."

She held the phone out to me, and when I took it, she crossed her arms and gave me a *fix this* look.

"Hi, yeah, I'm sorry about my behavior earlier. I guess I'm a little overprotective of Jennie."

"I can understand why you would be."

"Also, she showed me the sculpture. It's amazing... No, that isn't an adequate description. It's well, it's out of this world."

He was silent a moment before I heard him take a deep breath that he let out slowly. "I wanted to see your face when I gave it to you." He sounded disappointed.

I sighed. "I'm sorry, Eli. I can understand why you wouldn't want me to have it, if you want to take it back." The significance of calling him by his name for the first time wasn't lost on me, and I hoped he could hear the sincerity in my voice, for Jennie's sake if nothing else.

"No, it's yours. It's always been yours, even before I met you, if that makes any sense. Okay, let Jennie know I'll pick her up tomorrow then?"

I looked at Jennie and she was clearly still angry, and a tear had slipped down her cheek.

"She heard you," I replied, and without saying anything else, he hung up.

"I fucked this up!" she said. "I wouldn't be surprised if he fired me now."

"I... Jennie, I don't think you fucked anything up. I think it was just circumstances and surprise. I was the one who messed it up, although I didn't know you two were coming, so there's that."

Jennie got up and walked toward the door. "I'm sorry, Uncle Crea. I think I need to go work this out with him before I get fired and lose the most important thing I've ever done."

"I'm sorry, Jennie," I said as I followed her out the front door.

"Yeah, me too," she said, and walked to the Jeep, crawling into the driver's seat.

When she was gone, I collapsed onto my sofa feeling drained. I could see the sculpture on my table and couldn't resist going to take a closer look at it. It was magical, like looking at a Monet or a Rodin. You couldn't help but be drawn to it, admire it, and let it burrow into your soul.

I wasn't a huge art fan. In fact, I rarely ever participated in the San Francisco art scene, but even I could tell when something was spectacular, and this piece really was. As I stared at it and took in the intricate designs and delicate carvings, I began to believe maybe this actually was worth what Jennie's mom had said. That was enough for me to know I'd never be able to accept the gift, especially after what had happened and how I'd treated him.

The question was how to return it without being an even bigger asshole.

I lay down on my sofa again and, to my surprise, I drifted off.

I saw my grandmother staring at me from across a wide-open expanse covered with stumps. Despite the distance between us, I could see—feel—the sadness on her face.

I was shocked that I understood her when she spoke, her voice as strong as if she were standing in front of me. "I told you he was the key. You knew the curse was interfering, and now all may be lost."

I opened my eyes and was engulfed in feelings of loss and sadness... and my grandmother's despair. I texted Jennie asking if we could meet before they left town, but she texted back saying it wasn't a good idea. I *had* to talk to them, to Eli.

I called my brother, Lance, after giving myself a few moments to calm down. When I explained how I'd bungled everything with Eli and then Jennie, he sighed. "Crea, man, it's hard enough that Jennie's floating between our family and hers. Why didn't you try to call me or something before you jumped to conclusions?"

"I don't know. Shit, it was all out of the blue. You have to admit, it's strange, a guy I met only once showing up on my doorstep with my niece in tow. I rushed to judgment, and well, I... damn, Lance, you know how it is when we are around men we like..." *Like.* I couldn't deny it, I did find the man attractive, despite how shitty I'd treated him. And it all scared the shit out of me.

"Linda called and told me she thought they'd given you a sculpture."

"Yeah, that's actually why I'm calling. I can't accept it, even if I hadn't been a total ass. It needs to be in a museum or something, not on my dining room table."

"I think you're insane giving an Eli Bane back to Eli Bane. That man's sculptures are amazing, and there are rich people all over the world begging to commission pieces from him."

"He should sell this to one of them. Seriously, Lance, I can't accept this."

Lance let out a resigned sigh on the other end. "Want me to fly down and drive it back with you?" he asked.

"Well, I would if you were closer, but no, I don't want you to fly all the way here just to watch me pull my foot out of my damned mouth."

He chuckled. "You should have enough experience doing that by now anyway."

"Yeah, rub salt in my wound by making fun of me. That's what I need."

"Just trying to help, little brother, just trying to help."

"Well, stop trying! Well, okay, stop trying after you get me an address to drive this back to. Oh, and just so you know, Crater Lake National Park is confirmed. You and Kyle need to let me know when you're gonna be available, but keep in mind the park closes early because snow is intense in that area. I think we only have between June and September to visit."

"I'll find out Eli's address. You text Kyle and me, and all three of us can talk. Well, if Kyle is anywhere near civilization, that is. If you want us all to get away before September, you better text that now. Knowing our brother, he's probably in some jungle down in South America or something."

"True, okay, I'll text you both now."

Being Sunday, I normally would've taken the day off, but since I was going to end up having to drive back to Oregon and straighten all this out, I went into the office and made sure all my tasks for the week ahead were done. I was lucky as shit it was still early in the season, or I'd never get away with taking this much time off.

I steadied myself and sent a text to my boss, letting her know I'd be gone for a couple days due to a family issue. To my surprise, she texted me right back, saying it wasn't a problem.

Must be meant to be, I thought, then remembered my grandma's face from the dream.

I drove home thinking about my niece and the handsome man I'd treated with such disrespect. It was not like me to be so nasty. Even in the past, when my father's curse had interfered, I'd never been so angry, so volatile with anyone, but the anger and hate were... well, intense.

That's when my thoughts drifted to my father. "Fuck you!" I beat my hands on the steering wheel. All the feelings I'd had for Eli now circled back to the man who'd caused this. "Fuck you..." I said again, this time quieter, my fight gone and replaced with the intense sadness I felt every time I thought of Dad.

By the time I got home, I was shaking. I'd figured out that my reaction to Eli had been driven by my father, or his curse at least. It'd taken my natural skepticism and magnified it to the point that I felt unfounded rage. *You will never know the love of another man.* Was this how that wretched curse manifested itself? I would never know love because it prevented me from trusting good men?

I hated that it had so much power over me and had managed to influence my psyche. Not sure how to explain that part to Jennie or Eli, I knew I had to at least try.

For the third time in as many months, I prepared to travel to Oregon. It didn't escape my attention that I was returning over and over to the place where my life had begun. What was strange, though, was I'd somehow managed to avoid actually going home.

Even when my grandma was alive, I barely went to see her. She and her roommate were more likely to meet me in San Francisco, or before that, Seattle. She seemed to know I needed to avoid all the sadness that had accumulated there and worked to spare me.

Mom and Dad had split up shortly after he'd cursed us, and formally divorced sometime later. She remarried an evangelical preacher in Texas, but it didn't last long, and she had divorced him too. Dad, well, I had no idea what was going on with him. The curse my brother had thrown back on him had pretty much ended any concern or affection we might have once felt for him.

Now it seemed like I was making up for all the times I'd missed coming out to the area. Surprisingly, I didn't mind as much as I thought I would. Oregon was beautiful, and Chemeketa exceptionally so.

I let my mind drift as I drove the familiar roads back toward Klamath Falls. I was tired of my San Francisco job. When I first took it, I was so excited to be involved in a ground-breaking urban agriculture scheme. The fact that San Francisco was one of the hottest real estate markets in the world, and yet the city had actively decided to preserve its precious real estate for agricultural practices, made it irresistible for someone like me.

I didn't know when I'd lost interest in the whole thing. This was my eleventh year working with the grants program, and although I still believed in the cause, I was thirsty for something different. Maybe something less administrative and more hands-on.

I shook my head to rid myself of the swirling thoughts. I was just in a funk. Breaking up with my latest boyfriend had been tough on me. I'd settled and knew I had. He was an ass, but he was consistent. I longed for something long-term, real commitment. I'd never been one for one-night stands, but whether it was my father's curse or my inability to find a good man, or maybe both, I'd been dating for more than half my life and had never been a relationship that lasted more than six months.

When I crossed the state line, finally getting cell coverage again, I pulled over and texted Jennie, telling her I was coming. I didn't want to surprise them the way they had me. I also told her I understood if they didn't want to see me, but I'd be returning the art because I didn't deserve it after the way I'd acted. If they weren't there, I'd leave it on their porch or something.

I put my phone away and drove on toward the address my brother had texted me.

I didn't receive Jennie's response until I was almost there. I heard the ping, but decided to ignore it. I already knew what it said, and I didn't give a shit. I wanted to make this right, and returning the piece felt important.

I got lost three times trying to find the house, if you could call it that, up in the deep woods surrounded by national forests.

GPS had no idea where it was, and frankly, it was blind luck that finally got me to my destination.

The road, when I finally found it, wound slowly to the top of a mountain, then the driveway, which looked more like a dirt forest road, wound up to a metal building with logs strewn about. The only reason I was able to find it was the mailbox at the end of the forest trail with Eli's address on it.

My niece was sitting outside the workshop, legs and arms crossed. She was the very definition of angry and imposing. She had definitely inherited those qualities from my brother. When he was angry, his entire body showed it.

I got out, opened the back door of my sedan, and began to remove the piece. She came over before I could take it out, and pushing me back, slammed the door.

"He doesn't want it back," she said. "And it's rude that you'd shove it in his face like this."

"I agree, but it's worse to keep something like this when I've acted like such a fucking idiot," I replied, and opened the door back up. She slammed it again, barely missing my fingers. "Jennie, this is not about you, it's about me and him. I get you're protective of him, and I get you're trying to keep me from hurting him, but you need to back off!"

My niece had always seen me as completely pliable. We made a huge deal out of ensuring she felt loved and secure in our family given our odd family dynamics, so my new authoritative attitude seemed to shock her. She looked at me for a few seconds and left, going into the workshop and leaving me alone in the driveway.

I turned to open the door again and just about jumped out of my skin when the lumberjack appeared in front of me, blocking the door.

"Fuck!" I yelled in shock.

He moved closer into my space, his energy vibrating with anger. I should've been afraid. Hell, he could've beaten me to a pulp. I wasn't weak by any means. I worked with my body and worked hard, but I was no competition against a man with rippling muscles so nicely set upon his huge frame.

I didn't back off. Instead, I looked squarely into his eyes.

We stood staring at one another for a good thirty seconds. Pure lust slowly replaced the anger...

That was enough to cause me to step back, but when I attempted to turn, Eli grabbed me, twirled me around and, pushing my back up against the car, kissed me hard, letting the anger flow through the kiss.

I couldn't resist, even if I wanted to. He was pure heat, pure sex, and I thought as my mind melted that I was being kissed by some sort of forest-dwelling Greek god.

When he released me, I saw in his eyes the fire that he'd just poured into my mouth.

"You'll keep it, god damn it, or I'll shove it up your ass!"

It physically hurt when his hard body pulled away from me. Almost like I was under a spell, I grabbed his huge forearm, twisted him back around and reaching up, I pulled him back down for another kiss. This time I was in control, and I willed myself to show him how sorry I was for being an asshole. I willed the kiss to show him how thankful I was he'd thought of me, and created such a beautiful masterpiece.

I could feel the anger that had been in him seconds earlier slide from his body as the kiss between us melted from aggressive to something more primal and needy.

When Eli pulled away this time, the fire had been replaced with need. I could deal with that, felt more comfortable with that.

I cleared my throat, willing my voice to work. "I'm sorry for how I acted, and I don't deserve the piece you created. I just took you to the hospital. Any decent person would've done that. Then, when you brought it…"

He placed his big arm on the top of the car, letting his body lean into mine.

In a soft voice that sent blood rushing into my already hard cock, he said, "It isn't something you deserve or don't deserve. It's just a gift, and it's meant to be yours. I don't care what you do with it, except you can't leave it here." He pulled back then, looking at me for a long, delicious moment with those dark brown, lust-filled eyes. "You should leave now before it's too late."

He walked back toward the door my niece had disappeared through. After stepping inside, he closed the door behind him.

I stared at the door for a long moment, then got back into my car. I was about to turn the key, but I was too worked up to be driving just yet. I picked up my phone and opened the message. Jennie's text was simple.

You shouldn't come.

This was all a fucking mess, and I was just going to make it worse by going in there. Maybe if my niece hadn't been here, I would've taken my chances, but I knew in my heart if I confronted the man again, there was going to be serious fallout, the kind my niece didn't need to witness.

I was considering turning the key again when an older but equally large man knocked on my window. I jumped like the pansy I was, but seeing the man was unlikely to be a threat, I rolled my window down.

"I understand you and this one"—he pointed toward the workshop—"have had a disagreement. I doubt he'll be able to work it out right now, but he probably needs to. I'm guessing you need to as well. Why don't you come on over to my place for dinner? Give him some time to cool off."

"Who are you?" I asked, trying to shake off my suspicious nature.

"I'm his friend."

I nodded. "Where is your place?" I asked.

The man walked around the front of my car and opened the passenger door. He sat down in the seat and said, "Head back down the driveway. I'm the next property over."

After the adrenalin left my body, I felt exhausted. Finally, we pulled up at the man's house, and he invited me in. I was truly not in the mood to visit, but seriously, I didn't know what else to do, so I followed him inside.

The log structure was beautiful. We immediately came into a wide-open area with windows looking out over a graceful slope that seemed to frame the forests around the property. There was a giant fireplace on one side with a nice fire banked inside it.

The entire house smelled like wood fire mixed with home-cooked meals.

The man walked toward the great room and pointed toward a leather recliner. "Have a seat," he said. When I did, he sat across from me. "So, I've heard a bit about what happened, but it seems there were parts left out. Wanna explain it to me?"

"Not really," I replied honestly. "I don't really know you."

He chuckled. "I'm guessing you didn't drive all this way not to explain yourself, Mr..." He waited for me to fill in my name.

"Crea Franklyn," I answered.

"Mr. Franklyn," he said. "I've known that man all his life, and when he's fed up with someone, they aren't going to be talking to him any time soon. If you want him to hear your side of the story, you better share it with someone who has experience getting through that thick skull of his."

I heard a chuckle and turned to see a small woman walk into the room. "Hello, Mr. Franklyn, I'm Indigo Chelsea, Lee's wife."

The big man hadn't told me his name, I realized as the woman introduced herself. Nor had I asked.

"Eli is a complex man, one who usually keeps to himself. He isn't one to open himself up to others, especially people he hasn't met or doesn't know. You have to understand, when he made that piece for you, he was giving you a part of himself, something he has—at least to my knowledge—never done before."

I looked at the couple, bewildered. "I'm just so confused about all this. I realize he wanted to thank me, I get all that, but he is one of the most renowned wood-sculpture artists of our time. Jennie's mom shared with me what that piece is worth, and to be honest, that's about six times what I'll make this year. It is a bit like overkill, isn't it?"

Indigo smiled and sat down on the loveseat with her husband. "Men are strange creatures, Mr. Franklyn, and men like Eli are even stranger. I can't tell you why he chose to make and give you that piece, but when you rejected it, it really hurt him."

I sighed and looked down at my hands. "I didn't reject the piece. I just thought... well, to be honest, I didn't think, I was just overcome with anger and made a bunch of unfounded assumptions. I didn't know who he was, just saw this man with my niece, and assumed—"

"You were protecting someone you loved," she finished for me. I nodded and looked up at the couple. "Well, we love him, and so you'll understand that until the two of you address this and work through it, I'm going to need to ask you to stay with us."

I looked at her, shocked. "What? Stay with you?"

Lee laughed. "He isn't gonna come around anytime soon, son. He needs at least another twenty-four hours to steam. Your niece is plenty mad at you too, so the way we see it, it's in your best interest to stick around, if not for him, for her."

"Wouldn't it be better if I stayed in a hotel?"

They both laughed. "The closet hotel is about an hour's drive from here," Lee said. "I doubt it would be any different for you to be an hour away, or all the way home. No, the only way this gets resolved is for you to be in his face."

"This doesn't feel right," I said. "I didn't come here to hurt him, or make him feel worse, and I sure don't want to be in his face. I think I should go."

Indigo stood up. "Mr. Franklyn, you know as well as I do there are other things going on between Eli and your family. I'm sure you and he have even shared similar dreams. It's my understanding your niece is having those same dreams. You are welcome to run from this, but I'm afraid if you do, there will be consequences that can't be undone."

She walked toward her kitchen and picked up a leather pouch that she placed it in my hand, then sat down and waited for me to open it.

When I did, I found a small green stone encased beautifully in wood. "You are known as the emerald, isn't that correct?" she asked, and I looked at her with shock.

"My grandma called me her emerald."

"She is here with us, has been haunting your dreams. I've been holding onto that since Eli's accident. You see, we knew you were coming," she told me. "The question is, are you going to be brave enough to work this out, or are you going to leave?"

I stared at the rough emerald in my hand. The wood surrounding it looked like it was ancient, and the stone, although still in its rough state, seemed to shine. My ring was becoming warm too, and I reached over with my other hand and touched it.

When I did, the woman smiled.

"Let me show you to your room," she said.

Chapter Eleven

Eli

I SHOULD'VE KNOWN HE was going to react like he did. Hell, if I thought someone was trying to hurt Jennie, I'd react the very same way and I'd only known her for a few weeks, but his rejection had hit me in the heart like an arrow.

I also knew the upset and anger I was feeling toward him was more than just me. I'd seen it in my dreams, been warned by them that I was going to be tested by this, and despite that, I wasn't able to resist the anger and frustration at how he'd reacted.

I expected it to be done with after leaving his home. Jennie was upset too, but I thought it was more to do with her being embarrassed and maybe feeling a little guilty about how things worked out. We'd driven the six hours back to the workshop mostly in silence.

That night, Lee and Indigo demanded we go to their home for dinner, and Indigo basically confirmed that my reaction was more than just being upset. "Aren't you concerned you're being manipulated?" she asked.

"Yeah, I'm concerned, but I also don't seem to have the ability not to feel what I'm feeling."

She nodded and said, "It'll work out, but you are going to have to work through your emotions."

I shook my head. "No, it's over. I've delivered the piece, and now I'm free."

She actually laughed at me. "You know it won't be that easy. You were warned if you finished that piece, you'd be challenged. He'll be coming. You and I both know it. I wouldn't be surprised if he doesn't show up tomorrow."

Something about that statement sent a rush of anger flowing through my entire being. I could almost see the darkness settling over me. Indigo looked concerned, but didn't try to touch me. I wrestled back the emotion, and when I had it under control again, she said, "This is the curse you are fighting. These emotions aren't yours." She picked up a leather pouch, and it looked like she was going to hand it to me, then thought better of it.

Her eyes took on the light that told me she was prophesying. *"You must fight this yourself. You are the tool to overcome this hatred. He is strong, but he's been hurt time and again. You must be strong for him, lend your strength to him. That's what's needed to overcome."*

She sighed, the light leaving her eyes along with her strength. "Damn," she said. "That really gets more exhausting as I grow older. Go, prepare yourself for his arrival. We'll keep Jennie here for now," she said. "You must work through this anger, so you don't attack him when he arrives."

I knew she was right. The anger was real, even if it wasn't mine. It seemed to possess me. I went back to my workshop, and used my hand planer to work out my frustrations on some rather gnarly pieces of wood for another project.

I could tell Jennie was concerned, and my desire to protect her kept me from letting the anger go. I was glad she wasn't with me in the workshop, that she hadn't come back with me when I left Indigo and Lee's place.

After a few hours' work, I cleaned up my mess, put the tools away and went home. Of course, the anger that continued to course through me kept me awake, sitting in the chair, and staring at the fire until I remembered the raven's feather. I pulled it out, laid it on the floor in front of my little fireplace, and said, "Well, if you can help, this would be the time to do so."

The feather lifted from the ground as if a wind was blowing it, then when it was at eye level, it seemed to explode in green light.

I was standing in a forest I didn't recognize. There was a waterfall, and I was in a cave behind it. The forest smells were all around, and with the exception of the water, all other sounds were muted.

I saw him lying naked on a blanket in the corner of the great cave. I went to him, the anger still coursing through me, but that anger was banked up against my lust. I was torn between aggression and wanting to press my own naked body against his. My lust won out, and when I knelt beside him, he pulled me into an embrace.

As our bodies entwined, the anger began to lose its hold on me as it was replaced with need.

I awoke hard and swollen. Where the anger had once been, now I only felt desire—hot, inconsolable desire.

I looked at where the feather had been. *I'm not sure how that helped, but at least I can do something about the situation at hand.* When I got into bed, I let my hand take over, relieving myself again and again. Still, the feeling of need and want quickly returned. I knew before this was over, I'd need to have him under me. It would be the only remedy for this kind of craving.

The next morning, I didn't go to the workshop. Instead, I walked through the forests adjoining Lee's and my properties. Ours backed up to state forest land, but both Lee and I had agreed not to harvest our trees, so it was clear where our land ended, and the state's began.

I stayed among the older trees, letting them help me navigate the anger and frustration. Forests always touched my soul and grounded me. Even with their help, I was still struggling between the desire to hit and destroy things, and the lust I'd experienced the night before.

By late afternoon, I was beginning to lose the fight, and anger was beginning to find purchase inside me again. I walked back to the workshop, intending to work off the frustrations again with the hand planer and gnarled wood when I saw a car coming up my driveway. I knew it was Crea the moment he pulled up, although I couldn't see him. It was like whatever possessed me was telling me he was here.

I walked toward the car, red anger blazing my trail, and saw Jennie step up and speak to him. She was angry too, but seeing her and experiencing my feelings for her caused the anger to lose some ground. I hesitated until I saw her stomp off, and found myself standing in front of him.

That which possessed me wanted me to attack, prompted me to damage him. Remembering the feather, the vision of lust and sexuality between us, I allowed those feelings to take over instead. I tried to warn him to leave, willed him to do so while I warred with the emotions that I neither understood nor controlled, but he wasn't afraid, didn't cower down.

His bravery gave me pause and magnified my natural attraction for him.

When he resisted me, the anger wanted to explode. I channeled it into a kiss, rough and edgy, hoping he'd feel the anger, hoping he'd see I was trying to control it. I pulled away from him then and intended to leave.

Instead, he twisted me around and kissed me back. His kiss was different, pliant, giving. He expressed himself in that kiss in the only way my brain could comprehend at that point.

When he pulled back, I yearned for him. The anger still there, banked in the back of my mind. I was unable to compete with the kind, sweet and gentle kiss he'd returned for my angry and aggressive one.

He had undone me with his reaction. It was like cold water on a flame. I was still unsteady, so I issued the only warning I could. "You should leave now before it's too late."

As I walked away, I knew he wouldn't go. I didn't want him to. I had the vision of the sculpture in his hands, and felt the anger give way again. I'd found the antidote—compassion. My own feelings of gratitude and compassion were stronger than the imposed emotions of this cursed anger.

Jennie looked up at me when I walked into the workshop, but neither of us spoke. I went to where I'd left the boards attached to the clamps and began to plane them. This time, it wasn't with anger, but with the feelings I'd had the night he came to meet me before I went into surgery. I let the emotions I'd felt so strongly take precedence over any other feelings within me as Jennie and I worked in silence.

I worked late into the night, and when I finally got home, I crashed on my bed. When I woke at dawn the next day, the anger was almost gone—almost. I showered and got dressed. I was about to leave for Lee and Indigo's house when I froze, sexual need coursing through me. Like a predator who knew his prey was never going to escape, I sensed I was about to have my prize. I just needed to take it, and it was mine.

Chapter Twelve

Crea

I DISCOVERED I LIKED the Chelsea family a great deal more than I thought I would. Their daughter showed up along with Jennie, and after my niece gave me a good piece of her mind, she hugged me and accepted my apology.

None of us talked about Eli. He was the elephant in the room.

After Indigo gave me the wooden amulet with the rough emerald, the ring I wore maintained a constant warmth. I could tell Eli was battling something, and throughout my sleep, I kept having visions that spanned everything from angry outbursts from people I couldn't quite see, to intense sexual dreams set in caves with waterfalls.

I woke up exhausted and more than a little horny. I wanted to taste that man's lips again. I couldn't help but think if I could just inhale him again, let him somehow hold me, even if it was rough, that things would be okay.

I got up earlier than the rest of the house, just as the sun rose over the horizon. The room Lee and Indigo had put me in was truly amazing, with multiple windows around the many sides. When I lay in bed, I could smell him, and knew he'd slept here for a long time and not long ago.

The urge to see him overwhelmed me, so I ended up leaving the little room, and going out into the forests.

I knew from growing up in Chemeketa there were mountain lions and bears here. Of course, I shouldn't be out in the woods this time of day, knowing that was when they hunted, but I almost felt like I was being pulled out of the house and into the forest. Maybe I should've been afraid, but I wasn't.

I let my instincts guide me. Although the sun was up, it had yet to reach the darkness under the heavy canopy, but it was like my feet knew where to go. I climbed to the top of the mountain Lee and Eli's places were built upon. When I crested the ridge, I headed down until I stood looking at a small log structure.

I knew it was his home. I could feel him, just as I knew he could feel me. Fear spiked along with my heart rate, prompting me to run, knowing I would be better off facing one of the bears or mountain lions than the man in that cabin. But fear was no match for my lust for him, for the need I had to touch him and feel his big rough hands on me.

Eli came out of his front door, and the two of us stared at each other for several beats. I didn't wait for him to come to me. Instead, I began walking toward him. When I reached him, I looked up at his freshly groomed face, and offered myself to him.

He pulled me into his body with force, kissing me roughly as he pulled me inside his home. I knew he was possessed with anger, knew I was up against a danger

I'd never faced before, yet, for reasons unknown, I still trusted him completely.

We threw off closed as we went and by the time we were in his bedroom, I was completely naked, completely vulnerable. We didn't speak, not with words. The only communication between us was made with our bodies, all touch, taste, passion, and lust.

He let his mouth wander down my body, while his hands explored me. I was obsessed with those hands, big and rough, with calluses that set off sexual explosions as they scraped against my skin.

He came back up to my mouth, and I pushed him down on the bed and crawled on top of him. I moved my body up to his face. As he watched me, his dark brown eyes never leaving mine, I fucked his mouth, moving up and down to an aggressive rhythm that seemed to be beating within each of us.

When I couldn't resist the craving of tasting his mouth again, I pulled off. I laid my body on top of his bigger, broader one, and let my mouth ravage his. He didn't resist, returning passion for passion.

Tasting myself just made my lust more intense, and when I deepened the kiss, he tossed me on my back, his body blanketing mine, grinding his cock against me.

I moaned. The feel of him seemed to be locking a piece of myself back in place that had been missing without my knowing it.

He assaulted my body with his mouth, sucking at my neck, moving down to my nipples, nibbling, sucking, and sending me into ecstasy. My moans grew louder, and like the wild I'd associated with him the day before, it felt natural but feral.

When his mouth found my cock again, he sucked me down hard until my cock hit the back of his throat. He rocked back and forth until I arched into him. I didn't think I could bear any more when he swallowed, sending a rush of sensations I'd never experienced before from a blow job through my body.

I could feel myself cresting, and not wanting it to end, I pulled his head back and leaned up off the bed to kiss him again.

He reached over, neither of us saying a word, and pulled a condom and lube out of his nightstand.

We both knew what the other wanted, and I had never wanted someone inside me like I wanted him in this moment. After he'd put the condom on, he lubed up, and while stroking himself, he lifted my ass into the air and began to assault my hole with his tongue.

Never had a man known where to touch me, known how to entice me, and we had yet to say a word. He began using his thumb to probe my hole, prepping me for his cock. His tongue continued its assault as his thumb slipped in, using the saliva as lube. I was unable to breathe. The ecstasy of him working that delicate area was almost more than my senses could bear.

When he lowered my ass back onto the bed, I automatically crawled onto all fours. He lubed his fingers and thrust them into me, continuing to prep me. I could hear him jacking off his cock while his other hand massaged my ass.

When he could tell I was pliable, he removed his fingers, placing his hand on the small of my back. I almost purred. There was nothing soft or gentle about it. He slipped his cock inside slowly, letting me get used to him, but the moment he was fully in, he began to pound me.

I thrust back, desperate to feel his cock, all of it, and wanting the rush, the heat, and the unrelenting thrusts.

His moan filled the room. The first words spoken were to tell me how hot my ass was, how tight it was. Knowing I was giving him pleasure was the greatest gift he could give me.

I was lost, wanting... no, needing him, begging him to thrust harder, give me all of him, nothing less than all would ever be enough.

He pulled out and roughly tossed me onto my back, and lifted my legs up. When he shoved himself inside me again, I saw stars.

"I'm going to own you," he said, and I moaned my confirmation. I wanted to be owned by him.

He fucked me so hard, so intense, and it felt like the world was righting itself with each snap of his hips.

When he shifted, ever so slightly, his cock hit my prostate, causing me to see stars again. With only a few more strokes, I came so hard it landed on his face as well as mine. He licked the cum that'd dripped down onto my mouth as he pulled out, then removed the condom and jacked off. Within seconds he was coming hard across my chest.

When he was empty, he fell on top of me and turned to kiss me, traces of my cum lingering in both our mouths. He pulled back and smiled, a naughty smile that sent shockwaves to my heart. He used his finger to swipe more of my cum into his mouth, then leaned down, licking the spot where his cum was mingled with mine.

He looked at me as if asking permission, and when I didn't resist, he thrust his tongue into my mouth.

When he pulled back, I sighed. "Fuck, that was hot!"

He rolled over on his back, chuckling, and pulled me against him.

I snuggled into him in a way I would've never done with a hook-up. This was so different, so right.

"I needed that," he said, and kissed my head.

"Yeah, me too," I replied.

We ended up falling asleep in each other's arms, another oddity considering we were still mostly strangers. Everything about us had been odd, though, from the moment I'd met him.

We woke up much later, and when we pulled apart, the cum that we'd ignored resisted our parting.

"I think we're gonna need a shower," I said, teasing.

He moaned in a sexy, sleepy tone. "Good, I've been going over all the different ways I want to have you again, and the shower was on the top of my list."

"Mmm, that sounds perfect to me," I replied, but neither of us moved.

Finally, reality began to settle in, and I said what was obvious. "You know all this is really weird, right?"

He chuckled. "Yep."

"I'm okay with weird, are you?" I asked.

"Oh yeah," he replied, and gently turned me onto my back and began kissing my neck. "I'm *really* okay with weird."

Chapter Thirteen

Eli

I HADN'T EXPECTED HIM to show up, but the moment I saw him, I knew I wasn't going to waste time talking. When he came up to me, I let my animal instincts take over. The sex was the best I'd ever had. Not that I pursued sex that often, but when I did, I couldn't wait to get away afterward.

Not this time, though. Sex with Crea was everything I wanted it to be—fast, hot, and sensual. After we both came, and he snuggled into me, all I wanted to do was hold him.

I slept better with him in my arms than I had in months, maybe the best sleep I'd ever had.

When we woke a few hours later, and he began to tease me about a shower, it felt like we'd been lovers all our lives. My heart was already attached to Crea, and although I didn't understand it, I sure as hell didn't mind it.

The sex earlier felt primal, almost animalistic. This time, it felt different, more sensual and deliberate than fueled by uncontrollable lust and need.

I pushed him back onto the pillows and began to kiss him again. I took my time exploring the skin of his neck, breathing in his smell, and tasting the salty sweetness of him.

He moaned as my tongue explored him, kissing gently rather than assaulting his mouth. I felt the internal shift from need to desire.

As I moved back down his body, I tasted the combined seed we'd left there earlier. Normally I would've been disgusted by it, but with Crea, I relished in all of what we were together.

His cock felt silky against my tongue as I began to suck him off again. I'd always been into oral, enjoying the feel of a cock in my mouth. I'd also enjoyed giving and receiving pleasure in the few three-ways I'd participated in, but I'd never want to share Crea. I wanted him for myself. He was mine.

At almost the moment that thought entered my mind, he moved his body into a sixty-nine position and took my cock in his mouth. I'd only done sixty-nine a couple of times and was ho-hum about it, but damn, this felt right and perfect.

I moaned around his cock, and began to thrust into him, matching his rhythm. When we were both on the edge, he pulled back and asked where the shower was. I pulled him into my bathroom and thanked the gods I'd had the foresight to install an oversized shower.

I turned the water on and tugged him in as it warmed up. I lathered us both up, enjoying watching him as I moved my hands over his smooth body. He took the soap and began to wash me, paying special attention to my crotch and ass.

Pushing me under the spray, he rinsed me off, then fell to his knees, sucking my cock into his mouth. I thanked the gods again, this time for the extra-large water heater as the warm water flowed over us as he worked my cock. His fingers began to explore my ass, and although I never considered myself a bottom, I enjoyed the sensation of his fingers probing my hole while his mouth worked my cock.

I moaned. "Crea, fuck, Crea, that is so fucking hot."

He pulled off and looked up at me. I'd blocked the water so I could watch him suck me without it pouring into his face. He smiled wickedly, and as he swallowed my cock deep into his throat, he thrust his finger all the way into my hole.

Finding my prostate, he began to massage it while moving his mouth more aggressively. "Fuck, Crea, I'm coming!" I yelled.

Even if he'd wanted to pull back, there's no way he'd have been able to because I emptied into his mouth before my words were out.

He leaned back, a look of smug satisfaction on his face.

"You look like the cat that swallowed the canary." I laughed.

"More like the bird that swallowed the worm," he teased, and squeezed my still hard cock.

I pulled him up and pushed him against the tiles. "I'll show you bird and worm," I said, and using my soap-slicked hand, began jerking him off as I thrust my body against his. He moaned and squirmed, calling my name over and over until his breath caught, and he emptied his seed on my hip.

"Fuck!" he yelled, then laid his head against my chest as he rode out his orgasm.

"My gods, you feel so good," I said as I finished milking his cock.

He didn't respond, but continued clinging to me, and I understood all he was saying without words. We were on quite a ride together, and it was fun, amazing, and overwhelming at the same time.

I finished washing him as he lay against me, and pulling the shower head down, I rinsed us off. Opening the door to my shower, I grabbed a large towel off the rack and toweled us both off.

I'd have picked him up if he hadn't already moved toward my bed. Following behind him, I finished drying myself, and he took the towel and dried his hair, then looked at me.

"This really is too much. More than I've ever had and more than I ever intended. It's just too fast, though. I feel like I'm about to explode, Eli."

I smiled, because I felt the same. "We're men. I'm sure you've hooked up before."

I saw his face fall, and I quickly corrected myself. "I know this is more, Crea. I'm not saying it isn't, but we don't have to make more of it than we're comfortable with. The good news is we can take it as it comes now and just enjoy each other. Whatever was spurring this on, the intensity and bizarre undercurrent, I think we've managed to kick it back for now."

He nodded and came to me for an embrace. As I put my arms around him and pulled him closer, I held him for a moment, then kissed his head.

"Did you spend the night at Lee and Indigo's?" I asked, and he nodded. "Well, I'm guessing they'll be wondering what happened to you."

He looked up at me. "I doubt they're wondering too much. Indigo seems to have a sixth sense."

I chuckled. "You have no idea."

We got dressed, and I drove us to the workshop. "Give me a minute. I'm going to go get Jennie and take her with us. I think we all need to talk."

He just nodded and waited as I went in. Jennie was working on some of the skills I'd told her to practice. She looked up and smiled when she saw me. "Things back to normal now?" she asked.

"Um, no!" I said, and then smiled. "Come on, I'm driving Crea up to Lee and Indigo's. I think we all need to chat."

Jennie looked surprised that Crea was with me. She came out and immediately noticed we both had wet hair. "You had sex?" she said, looking between us both.

Crea's eyes grew wide, and I couldn't help but laugh.

"Of course," I said, and climbed into the driver's seat of the ATV. "Climb in."

As we began to move, I heard her say under her breath, "Men!"

Chapter Fourteen

Crea

T HE ROLLERCOASTER RIDE THAT morning had been intense. There were so many forces at work, not least of which was intense attraction and sexual desire. Even if all the other stuff wasn't involved, it would have still been overwhelming.

The ride to Lee and Indigo's had been light, though. Even after Eli admitted to Jennie that we'd had sex, which was mortifying for me, she quickly came to terms with it, and chatted about all the woodworking stuff she wanted to learn.

I leaned back in the seat, not really following Jennie's chatter but enjoying my niece's excitement, and enjoying Eli's big, rough hand resting on mine even more. How could you like someone this much when you'd only just met them?

Indigo was setting the table when we arrived and, as I'd guessed, she smiled and gave Eli and me a wink when we sat down. She declined help, then set heaping bowls of breakfast goodness in front of us, along with a large pot of coffee.

All three of us went for the coffee, and I chuckled. "There's something about this part of the country and coffee." My niece smiled as she took the pot and poured herself a cup, then passed it to Eli, who passed it to me.

Indigo sat down but didn't eat anything, saying she'd already eaten. Lee came in a few minutes later freshly showered and sat down, and ate us all under the table.

"Eli," he said as he was buttering a very large biscuit, "I got notice from the Chemeketa council yesterday. I was going to talk to you last night, but, well, you were occupied." He winked at me before continuing. "As you know, the great forest's conservation worker has passed away, and they're looking for his replacement. They've asked me to sit on the selection committee, but I already know who that person is supposed to be."

Jennie, not catching onto who Lee meant, asked, "You mean the old-growth forest that surrounds Chemeketa? I thought that was some state park or something."

Lee smiled at her. "It's a public-private initiative. It's not officially a park, because it isn't intended for tourism. It's supposed to be reserved for the community."

He didn't elaborate, but I knew what he was talking about. My brothers and I hadn't participated in the rituals of Chemeketa, but our grandmother had, and she would sometimes tell us about them.

"You have to be a member of the religious order to use them, if I understand correctly," I said to Jennie.

Indigo shook her head. "No, we don't restrict its use to only those who practice our ways. There are areas that are restricted, just like in any spiritual environment, but those are protected, and unless you have permission, you probably won't even know where they are." She smiled then, took a piece of bacon, and nibbled on it.

"Anyway"—Lee smiled at his wife—"the forest must be guarded to keep people from poaching, but mostly to ensure we don't have a forest fire."

Indigo shivered. "That's the most important." She looked at Jennie and me, her expression turning serious. "Did you know Chemeketa is the only part of this area that didn't burn down in the eighteen forties with Westward Expansion?"

We both shook our heads.

She leaned back, clearly about to give us the story. "Long story short. A military cook by the name of Johnson deserted his vessel, which was headed to Portland, and traveled deep into the Willamette Valley to stake a land claim. The man brought nasty energy with him, and the Native peoples who lived there, although already devastated by disease, said they could feel him as he moved up the valley. While clearing the land, he set a wildfire which burned over one and a half million acres, and displaced the few Natives who'd survived the outbreak. Chemeketa was the only place spared, and most of us believe it was because of its spiritual nature. Regardless, we don't want to tempt fate. There's been a conservator on that land since our community began settling the region."

Lee turned to Eli and asked, "Are you able to come with me to the council meeting? It's tonight."

Eli glanced at me, a small smirk forming at the corner of his mouth. "I think I might be busy."

Both Lee and Indigo chuckled, and Lee responded with, "He can come too."

"I should probably get back home. I have work," I said.

Indigo looked sad. "I think you should call your employer," she replied.

I looked at her questioningly, and she just shook her head. "Remember, it isn't your fault. Things are in motion you have no power to control."

Her response unsettled me. I'd known enough of my grandmother's friends to know strange when I saw it, and it didn't usually bother me. Still, I always felt uneasy whenever I met someone who knew things they shouldn't have known. The fact that my job might be over, well, that made it worse.

"Excuse me," I said, and stepped outside.

My boss answered on the second ring. "Hello, Catalina, it's Crea. I thought I'd check in to see if there are any fires I need to put out."

I could tell by the way she hesitated that Indigo had been right, and something was up.

"Crea, I was going to wait until you were back to tell you, but our benefactor passed away. His wife contacted me yesterday and told me they won't be funding us after this month. I'm sorry I can't give you more notice, but I have to let you go. I'm so sorry, Crea. I'm writing your recommendation letter even as we speak."

"Shit," I said, then apologized. "Well, I didn't see that coming."

"None of us did. Apparently, the garden project was his lover's thing, and now that the old man is gone, his wife and lover are at war."

I sat for a moment thinking, then said, "I'm going to stay in Oregon for a while. I'll do my last two weeks when I come back, but can you make sure to let all the garden managers know? I don't have internet access here. Heck, I'm lucky to have enough bars for this call."

"I've already begun that email too. I'll let them all know you'll work with them next week on writing new grants and in helping them set everything up for this one to conclude."

"Thanks, Catalina, and don't feel bad. If this was going to happen, it's the best time for it."

"You're just trying to make me feel better like you always do, but I appreciate it nonetheless."

After hanging up, I sat down on the front stoop and stared out over the landscape. A few moments later, I heard the door open and knew it was Eli without having to look.

"Bad news?" he asked, sitting next to me.

"Well, if you consider being unemployed in one of the most expensive places in the country bad news, then yeah, it's pretty bad."

"You wanna come with Lee and me to see the old-growth forest in Chemeketa?" he asked.

"Yeah, I sort of do. I took the week off anyway. I'd rather do my final two weeks after everyone's had enough time to deal with the news, so I can at least be semi-productive with what time I've got left."

"I'm glad you're coming. Indigo's a hedge witch, and she just told us you should really come with us, not that I'm committing to anything. I have no desire to work for a committee for any reason." He shook his head like he was in pain.

I laughed. "Why? Bad experiences?"

He nodded. "I was asked to do a consignment piece a few years back for a nonprofit up in Seattle. They wanted it to have an indigenous flair to it, but modern and traditional and... well, let's just say all eleven board members had an opinion, and those opinions weren't even similar. By the time I'd wasted weeks trying to hash out what they wanted, I had to put my foot down and say I'd make it, and if they wanted it great, if not, I'd sell it to someone else. I swore after that I'd never work for another committee again."

"Did they buy it?" I asked, intrigued.

"Yep, and said I'd caught everyone's vision, which was literally impossible."

I laughed. "Eli?"

"Yeah?"

"Mostly, I just want to do what we did this morning—a lot. So, can we plan on getting our own rooms, and preferably in a totally different hotel from my niece?"

He leaned back and laughed, a deep and glorious sound that sent goosebumps across my skin. I was one hundred percent sure I'd never felt so attracted to someone as I was to him.

"I think that's wise," he said, once he'd recovered.

"I've always had committees to answer to. The secret is to know when they've made a definitive decision and when to ignore the rubbish."

"I'm not playing," he said. "I like my life just like it is."

I was surprised when his large arm slipped around my shoulders, and even more surprised when I laid my head against him, feeling strange and yet strangely comfortable. "You'll know what's right. Meanwhile, I've got to figure out what I'm gonna do with my life." I looked up at him and smiled. "Know anyone looking for an urban agriculture organizer?"

He kissed the top of my head. "Nope, but Che's full of hippie folk. I'm sure they've got plenty of people looking for that kind of thing."

I pulled away. "Yeah, but I pretty much decided I was never moving home. When I left, I meant to stay gone."

"The entire West Coast is hippie country. I'm sure you'll be fine."

"You know urban farming isn't just for hippies. Lots of people have little gardens. I could show you how."

He laughed. "I get plenty of fresh fruits and veggies from Indigo and her hedge friends. I'm pretty sure I'm not a 'planting in the soil' kind of person."

"Your loss," I said and stood up to go back inside. It'd been a long time since I'd felt so comfortable with someone, and the fact that we were chatting as if we'd already known each other for months felt even more strange, like we'd entered the twilight zone or something.

We ended up leaving for Chemeketa together. I decided to drive my own car, and Jennie and Eli rode with me while we followed Indigo and Lee. It was a three-hour drive from their part of the world to Chemeketa, but it felt like only a few minutes with the conversation flowing between the three of us. Jennie was completely enthralled with Eli, and they talked about woodworking most of the time.

I could tell Eli wasn't used to talking that much, and at one point, he looked exceptionally tired, so I took over the conversation and asked Jennie about her mom and dad, then the stuff I knew she liked to talk about. Her favorite subject, of course, was my brother, her "sperm daddy" as she called him, and how he needed to find someone to love, someone better than the loser he'd been married to who ended up cheating on him. We'd kept the curse a secret from her and everyone, so she wouldn't have known him finding everlasting love was unlikely for many reasons.

We pulled up to what I vaguely remembered was the old meeting hall called the Grange House. It was built in the style of a church with a huge hall and big windows on the side to let the light in. I remembered from my school days learning that the granges were a nineteenth century thing uniting farmers for lobbying efforts. My grandmother had dragged us boys down to this old Grange House over the years for community gatherings. We had an old Presbyterian church in Chemeketa, but because the entire town was comprised mostly of pagans, the Grange House tended to be the place people gathered.

The Grange House sat right on the edge of the great wood, at least that's what my brothers and I called it. It was about five miles from Grandma's home. Whenever we went to the Grange House for a potluck or the multitude of festivals the town celebrated, we'd climb up into the woods with the kids our age to hang out, hidden from view of the adults.

We climbed out of the car and were immediately met by an ancient-looking man. As I looked closer, I thought he looked familiar, but I couldn't remember his name. He grabbed Lee into a hug, which was comical considering the man was about half the height of Lee. He smiled and waved at Indigo, then when he got a look at Eli, they both laughed and embraced. When the old man noticed me, though, he froze.

"I can't believe it. I didn't think I'd see the day when one of the Franklyn brothers returned."

I smiled at him, and said, "I'm sorry, it's been a long time. You'll have to remind me of your name."

The old man chuckled. "I doubt you ever knew it. I'm Katan Manning. I'm the mayor of our little town here."

I nodded and smiled. I didn't dare admit I thought Chemeketa wasn't big enough for a real mayor. My grandmother had held the title, but I'd always thought it was basically an honorary position. Mr. Manning turned back to Eli, and said, "Well, we all think you're the man for the job. Might as well come on in and meet the rest of us."

"Whoa," Eli said. "I've got a job. I only came to keep Lee company and visit the old forests again. I'm definitely not your man."

The older man chuckled. "If you say so, son," he said, and led us into the Grange House.

I smiled at Eli's discomfort. Just by the way everyone was acting, I guessed they were all resolved he'd be the one who'd take the job. I didn't know Eli well enough to know either way. Still, I knew from our earlier discussion he was unlikely to want to deal with a committee making decisions. Having dealt with the San Francisco government for all these years, I knew city councils were the worst kind of committees.

The old Grange House brought back fond memories. I could almost taste the apple pies and tarts that adorned every potluck our grandma had dragged us to. By dragged, I meant literally, sometimes by the ear. She was very liberal, and thought we should be free to explore as we saw fit, but when the town had celebrations, we were expected to attend. We almost never wanted to, but looking back now, those occasions were among my most treasured memories.

A small group of older people sat on metal folding chairs near the old stage. From the look of them, not one was younger than sixty. I smiled as I thought they'd all be people my grandma would've been friends with, and the thought brought on such intense grief, I had to stop and catch my breath before going over to them.

As soon as we neared the group, a woman about my grandma's age caught sight of me, and we immediately recognized each other. "Donna Rummel?" I asked.

She got up, walked over, and pulled me into a hug. "Boy, where have you been all these years?" she asked. "I've missed seeing that handsome face of yours."

I smiled. Donna had been one of Grandma's besties and she'd hung out at her house all the time while we were growing up. Donna was full-out naughty, and in fact, she was the first to slip Lance a joint, long before it was legal. Even our grandmother, hippie that she was, would've frowned at that.

Before Donna and I could catch up, the old man, Mr. Manning, called the group to order. "Let's get this going, so we can all get home before it starts raining again."

I hadn't noticed it looking cloudy, but I knew from experience the weather in this part of the world could change in a moment as the ocean sent its mists into the woods surrounding the town.

"As you know, Lee Chelsea promised that when Mr. Ellefson passed, he'd help us find a new forester."

It was all I could do not to laugh when all the old people turned and looked at Eli. He squirmed in his seat next to me.

"Lee, would you like to say something?" Mr. Manning asked.

"Hi, all, I know you're all mourning the loss of Mr. Ellefson. As you know, he and I were close friends, and we spoke on many occasions about who he wanted to be his replacement." Lee looked at Eli then and smiled, but had the good grace not to put him on the spot. "I have his request, but I'd like to spend some time at the property to make sure our decision feels… right," he concluded.

"Are you wanting to stay in the cabin?" Donna asked.

Lee nodded. "I think it would be best to be in the heart of the old forest, don't you?" he asked, and she nodded.

"I've been watching the old place, but it's a lot for an old woman like me. I hope we're able to fill his position sooner rather than later."

Without looking, she reached across me and patted Eli on the knee, and the large man blushed like an embarrassed teen.

I couldn't resist the chuckle this time, which earned me an annoyed look from Eli.

"Good. Donna, if you'd give Eli the keys, then they can stay there tonight. Meanwhile, we need to discuss the new community gardens," Mr. Manning said. "As was discussed in our last meeting, many of us are getting too old to manage our gardens, and we don't have young people living with us to take care of them like they used to, so we should discuss using the acreage around the Grange House as a community garden."

Donna sighed. "We should have the Earth Guild appoint the job, but I can't imagine who'd do it. They're just as old as this group is. All the younger ones have their own farms to tend."

I didn't move. If I remembered correctly, Donna was smart as a whip and intuitive as well. Maybe not as much as Indigo, but if she detected even the slightest discomfort, she could always sniff down the root cause.

"Next meeting, we need to have the Earth Guild here then. Donna, since you're the representative for the Earth Guild, we'll leave that up to you," Mr. Manning said, and Donna nodded. "What we can do today is vote for the salary we discussed last week. All those in favor of a monthly stipend to manage a community garden around the Grange House, please say aye."

All five council members did so. "Now, what I was thinking is we'd need to have the salary be the same as what we're paying the forester. That's more than we'd normally consider since this person is only going to be working part-time, but I'll remind you all that, unlike the forester, we won't be providing housing."

Mr. Fox, an ancient man I remembered from my youth who looked like Treebeard from *The Lord of the Rings*, said, "The forester has to maintain the cabin though, and it's not like we provide any funding."

"That's true, and thank you, Mr. Fox, but remember we do have an allowance for the property for any large expenses and management." The mayor looked sideways at Eli, and it was clear he was trying to make it sound more appealing to him.

They discussed the annual salary for the position, and I was surprised by the amount. They were actually paying a little more than I was making in San Francisco, and I knew for a fact the living expenses here were much less than in the city.

"Excuse me," I heard myself say. "What's the job description for the position?"

I saw Indigo smile out of the corner of my eye and ignored her. I needed a job, and if this could be it, the hell if I wasn't going to consider it, especially at that rate.

Donna cleared her throat, and when I looked over, she had a sly smile on her face too. "We haven't discussed that yet, but we do know we want to grow enough vegetables and fruit to match what us older folks would've grown for ourselves. We'll have to meet with all the community members to see what their annual needs are."

"I don't mean to interrupt, but will there be individual plots, or are you just planting row crops?"

"That'll be up to the manager to decide," Donna said. "What we do know is we want the retirement community that's being built on the other side of the road from the Grange House to have direct access to the food."

I nodded and said thank you, feeling my face blush. What the hell was I doing? Now Donna was going to harass the shit out of me. The woman was a master at doing that when she wanted something.

When the meeting concluded, Mr. Manning came over and pulled me into an embrace similar to how he'd greeted Eli and Lee. "It's good to have you home, son. Go talk to Donna about that position, it looks like you might be interested."

I smiled, but kept my mouth shut. I didn't know what the hell I wanted.

The group all appeared to know Lee, Indigo, and Eli, and they spent several minutes talking to each other and being introduced to Jennie. Donna broke away from the group and looped her arm into mine. "I know you didn't mean to spill that many beans, but you know how much I love a good bean soup. Why don't you ride with me up to the old cabin, and I'll fill you in on the details of the job."

"Donna, I—"

She stopped me midsentence. "You aren't committing to anything, I get it, but you do need to know what it is before you can decide, correct?"

I just nodded. I was numb. Today had been too much, and I was beginning to crash emotionally.

I gave my keys to Eli and got into Donna's ancient Ford F-150 pickup. The others followed us as she led the way through the old forest for what felt like forever, climbing the steep cliff roads to the cabin.

"So, what have you been doing these past few years?" she asked the moment I closed the door and put my seatbelt on.

"I, um..." I was hesitant to tell her, considering I was probably the perfect candidate for the job. "Well, I've been in San Francisco most of this time working as an urban agriculture organizer. I was in the North Seattle area before that, working in the farming industry up there."

Donna chuckled. "It's still fun. Chemeketa brings us the people we need when we need them."

"Wait, Donna, I've been gone from here so long, I... well, I never intended to come back. This is a fluke."

She looked at me for a moment, and asked, "Do you still have your job in San Francisco?"

I sighed. "Well, that's not the point."

She laughed out loud. "When did your job end?"

I couldn't help but smile. "I refuse to answer that."

She patted my knee, much like she'd done with Eli earlier. "It's okay, honey, you've got time to get used to the idea. Meantime, why don't you meet the Earth Guild the day after tomorrow at ol' Jack Henry's farm. He's treating us to a fresh breakfast. That man has been so lonely since his husband died last year, so we tend to meet there when we can. He can also cook better than the rest of us."

I smiled. I didn't remember a Jack Henry or his husband, but I hadn't spent much time getting to know people in Chemeketa. After going away for college, I only returned home during school breaks and even then, usually stayed put at Grandma's house. By twenty-one, I was fully on my own.

"So, what is the Earth Guild?" I asked.

She thought for a moment. "I don't know what all your grandmother taught you. Seems like you boys were only here for a moment, then you were gone, but you know there are four elements, right?" she asked.

I nodded. "Air, Water, Fire, and Earth."

"That's correct. All four elements have their own guilds in Chemeketa, and each group is in charge of their section. We are responsible for the Guild House and the forest."

"That's cool, I guess. Different from the rest of the world, but cool."

Donna chuckled. "You really don't know your heritage, do you?"

I frowned. "Donna, you know our story. I'm sure Grandma filled you in on our parents. They wanted to be politicians, so they gave up this life. By the time we ended up here, like you said, we were gone too soon to learn much."

"Why did you stay away?"

"Pain in remembering," I answered honestly. Of course, the fact that we were basically backcountry driving and I was bouncing all over the place made it difficult to hide anything even if I wanted to.

Donna didn't seem to be affected by the drive in the least. "Sometimes not remembering can be more painful," she said. "Your grandma missed you terribly. Not that you should feel guilty, she was also a wild and free woman who did what she pleased. She respected you boys and your need to be away. I wish I was a lesbian. I'd have married that woman in a heartbeat."

I laughed out loud at the comment, but Donna didn't crack a smile. "Did you have a woman crush on my grandma?"

"I did, but we both liked men. It's a shame. I'm coming back as a straight man next time, and I'm gonna chase her down and marry her, as the gods are my witness."

I smiled. "I'm glad she had you. I know you two had a lot of fun together."

"I miss her about every day. Well, mostly, she's been by a few times. Have you seen her yet?" Donna asked.

I smiled. "Too often. I swear she's haunting my dreams."

"She's probably haunting you, period. She wanted to clean things up with you and your brothers and what your dad did to you all. I'm guessing she's doing that now. Things are supposed to be clearer from that side of the veil."

I shook my head. "Seems like it'd be more difficult."

Donna just shrugged. "None of us know, at least, not until we're there."

We pulled up in front of one of the most impressive cabins I'd seen in years. It was large, two stories, and looked as if it'd been built in the nineteen twenties in the same architectural style you'd expect to see in a national park. A wide porch wrapped around the cabin, and when Donna walked me around the back, we were treated to an amazing view of the ocean off in the distance. The cabin sat on top of an odd, jutted rock formation that I assumed was left over from when it was an active volcano. There were cliffs around the property that gave it a panoramic view of the surrounding old-growth forest. I'd spent some time out East in the pine forests, and remembered the tall fire lookout towers built to keep an eye on the forests. In a way, it was like that, but with considerably more style.

The cabin interior wasn't quite as noteworthy. The home looked well-maintained, but nothing appeared to have been updated since the nineteen sixties. The avocado fixtures were a really good indication of that. Despite the age, you could tell at one time this had been quite a spectacular place. The word that kept coming to my mind was *groovy*.

Donna looked around and smiled. "Don Ellefson hasn't updated this place since his wife died in nineteen seventy-six. I suspect the electrical needs updating, and there's a little money in the budget to help, but that's officially supposed to be for the roof and structural needs. However, we can allot some of that money for a remodel. Lord knows it needs it."

She peered into the kitchen, and a look of nostalgia crossed her face. "I sure had some wild times up here when we were young, though. Freda knew how to throw a good party. Anyway, you all make yourselves at home. All the sheets are clean. I had the Earth Club from the local high school come up after Mr. Ellefson died and help me do a thorough cleaning." She looked at me then and smiled. "No need to worry, he passed in the hospital down in Tillamook, and he's transitioned to be with Freda. As far as we could tell, there are no remnants of his spirit here."

The group walked in as Donna finished her tour. We all brought our bags in, and each took a room. When I came back downstairs after looking over the place, I asked Donna if the Ellefsons had any family, and who was going to get all this stuff.

She shook her head slowly. "Freda died during childbirth, and Don didn't remarry. He had a few nephews and nieces, but they're almost as old as me. No, there isn't anyone to take his things. Whoever takes his place as the forester will have to go through their belongings and donate what they don't want."

Donna left us shortly after that. Eli and Lee went out and got several dried-out logs to put into the old circular fireplace in the middle of the living room. It was so bizarre, I'd seen something similar when I'd watched *White Christmas* as a kid, but I didn't think anyone still had them. From the look of it, the fireplace had been used frequently.

We sat around the campfire-like setting and enjoyed the quiet. I was exhausted from a day of ups and downs that started way too early, so I didn't last long before I excused myself, drifted up to my room, and fell asleep.

I'll admit, I was disappointed the next day when I woke up and Eli wasn't in my bed. I guessed it was because we had a full house, though. In the kitchen, I found a newer coffee pot, which surprised me, since I'd almost expect-ed to find an old percolator like the one my grandma had.

There were fresh supplies as well, like a new can of coffee, not the fancy kind, but people in the middle of a forest on the top of an extinct volcano couldn't be choosers.

I got the coffee ready and turned it on. I was about to peruse the cupboards for any evidence of breakfast fixings when Indigo appeared behind me, making me jump.

She chuckled at my surprise and took my place in front of the refrigerator, pulling out eggs, bacon, and some fresh broccoli.

"Morning," she said.

I was clearly being dismissed, so I went over to the old kitchen island with equally old stools, and sat down to watch her.

"Did you sleep well?" I asked.

She nodded. "It's a good house. It's almost like you're embraced here. Can you feel it?" she asked as she put the bacon into a frying pan she'd found inside the ancient oven.

"I can feel this place has been loved. It just feels... like home."

She smiled as she cracked the eggs into a bowl she'd found next to the sink.

"I think one could have a nice family up here, if you were looking for such a thing," she said, not looking at me as she stirred the eggs.

"I suppose if someone was looking for that, and willing to do a lot of updating and remodeling, it would be perfect."

I knew I was being questioned, but I didn't feel like playing. The intensity of the day before had worn me out, literally, and I wanted a day away from thinking about work, relationships, grandmothers, and fathers who would curse their own children. All of it.

Luckily, I didn't have to get much more of the third degree before the rest of our crew began to show up. By the time everyone was settled, Indigo was ready to serve the food.

"You love to do this, don't you?" I asked as she dished a large helping of scrambled eggs onto my plate.

Indigo just smiled. "Everyone has their own hobbies. I love to cook and tend to all the domestic chores of keeping house. I grew up in a very modern home, with a mother who was liberated long before that was popular. I got to choose this, because I loved it, not because it was expected. Lee was always smart enough to appreciate my efforts and see them for the value they are."

"Yes, that's true," he said. "Any man who'd act like this isn't a massive gift is an idiot. I may be a lot of things, but I'm not an idiot."

I grinned. It always felt good to see a couple who'd figured out how to navigate all the pitfalls life put in front of them. Of course, I'd never had that kind of relationship, but it sure felt good to see one that worked.

Once everyone finished eating, Lee, Indigo, and Jennie headed into town, while Eli and I hung back at the cabin.

"So, you're on the spot, huh?" I asked, wanting to offer him a little comfort if possible.

"Not really. I figured they'd ask me since I was close to Don. He used to let me ramble through the woods to find fallen limbs and timbers to use in my early woodworking projects."

"Really?" I asked. "You used sticks in your early projects?"

Eli laughed. "No, there are some very large trees, some almost the size of the redwoods in California. They sometimes drop massive limbs the size of normal trees. When they do, you can use them without cutting trees down for projects like the one I made you."

The tension in the room climbed about a hundred percent, and I sighed. "We should probably talk about that, huh?" Eli shrugged, so I took a deep breath, and said, "When I saw you with Jennie, it freaked me out. I'm usually very open and avoid conflict. In fact, I'm more likely to give someone a chance who doesn't deserve it, but when it comes to my family, I'm fierce. Too fierce, I'm afraid." I looked down at my hands, and Eli remained silent. "Okay, so it's also my pride." I looked up and into beautiful eyes that seemed to be taking me in. I had to look away so I could continue instead of crawling into his lap, which was what I really wanted to do. "When I found out what your piece was worth, it sort of startled me. You know I don't make enough in a year to buy that piece from you. I don't make enough in three years to buy it."

"Well, that worked out, since I wasn't selling it to you," he said, and I could feel his frustration returning.

"Eli, it was an amazing gift. Something I wouldn't have imagined. You are amazing too. It was just a lot to take in all at once, but I've thought a lot about it, and I've decided I'm going to accept it, because one, I can tell you really meant for me to have it, and two, even if this doesn't go anywhere, I want to remember how it felt for someone like you to make love to me the way you did."

Eli seemed to be mollified. He looked through the sliding glass doors out toward the ocean, and said, "I kept having visions of what that piece would look like. The log that fell on me, at first I wanted to destroy it, chip it into a million pieces and burn each of them one by one, but then I began to envision what it would look like if I molded it, changing it from something so destructive to something that could be appreciated. I knew the moment I met you in the hospital, I was going to make you that piece."

He paused a moment, as if lost in thought remembering that difficult time, before continuing. "As I healed, what it would look like became clearer and clearer. Then, Jennie came along, and she had the perfect skill level and patience to work through all the parts and help me put it together. I didn't know she was your niece, but it doesn't surprise me. That piece was yours the moment you picked me up from the side of the road, and the fact that your family came to me to help me build it only makes sense."

I came over and stood in front of him. The moment he slipped his arms around me, I felt the familiar glory of being in his embrace.

"I love how you smell," I said.

"What?" he asked, and I felt the vibration of his chuckle.

I pulled back to look into his eyes. "I love how you smell—all woodsy, like you'd think a lumberjack should smell."

He shook his head. "You smell like home," he said, confusing me.

"Like home?" I asked.

He nodded. "I grew up on a farm. Well, really it was a vineyard, but we didn't call it that. It was just the farm. When my father worked the land between the vines, the earth gave off a rich, deep smell that reminds me of home. When I'm with you, I catch just a whiff of that earthy smell, and it makes me think of my childhood home."

I wasn't sure how to take that. "Is that a good thing?" I asked.

He pulled me closer and sniffed my neck, and goosebumps broke out across my body. "It's a *really* good thing," he said.

Chapter Fifteen

Eli

WE WERE WALKING DOWNSTAIRS just as the crew came barreling into the house. Jennie looked at our wet hair and shook her head. "You two fuck like rabbits," she said, and Crea did the obligatory 'Jennie, stop that,' and blushed all the way up to his ears.

Gods, he was so cute. Indigo had brought the makings for hot dogs and smores, and I got a fire going again. "So, what do you think of the job offer?" Lee asked.

I just shook my head. "I haven't thought about it really-ly," I said.

Lee studied me for a moment, like he did when he knew I was lying, but didn't push it any further.

Indigo, however, didn't hold back her thoughts. "It's a beautiful spot, but your workshop is three hours from here. How would you do your art? And would being the forester impede your ability to spend hours on your projects?" She looked at me and Lee without backing down. I could tell she had a strong opinion about me not doing my woodworking any longer.

Lee shook his head. "There's room in town for the sawmill and studio. In fact, there used to be a sawmill in that spot in the nineteen thirties before the town drove them out. This town was full of environmentalists even back then, and they've always hated all the tree cutting around here. They've called it scalping the mountains since I was a kid."

"It does seem harsh," Jennie said.

Lee shrugged. "What's the difference between growing trees and growing crops? In the Midwest, they grow corn every year and chop it down, depleting the soil and causing intense runoff in the process. At least forestry keeps the streams clean and replenishes the forests after they're cut, all of which is good for the environment."

I could tell a long, drawn-out argument was coming, so I said, "If I were to consider the job, I'd have to have access to the forest and be able to cut up the dead trees. I know the purists like to leave the trees to rot naturally, but Indigo's correct in that I have my art. I'm not willing to trade that to be the forester, even if it is the forest I've loved since childhood."

Lee smiled. "I doubt they'd let you take all the dead trees, but there's more than you could ever use here anyway. Besides, you can probably use a lot of the discarded lumber from the forest industry, like you were doing up by Diamond Lake when you crushed that leg of yours."

I squinted at Lee. He'd barely brought the incident up since it happened, so I knew he was leveraging that for his sales pitch.

"I don't know. I like the idea," I answered honestly. "But, it'd be different, not to mention I'd have the city council breathing down my neck."

Lee laughed. "They meet once a month. They're all over sixty, and Old Man Ellefson trained them long ago not to micromanage. I doubt you'd even know they're there unless you neglect your duties, which I know would be impossible for you."

"Lee, there's a lot to manage here. The summers are getting dryer and dryer. They probably need to work with the state to manage the underbrush, and figure out how to lower the risks of a summer wildfire. If I spend all my time on things like that, I can promise you I won't have enough time to do any art. This really would be a full-time job."

Indigo looked over at me and back to Lee, and said, "Tell him."

Lee looked perturbed. "I didn't plan to do that until he made up his mind."

"Then I will. Are you willing to take the job right now?"

I felt like I was being backed into a corner, and crossed my arms defensively. "No, I don't have time to do it and continue with my art like I want to."

"What if you had help?" she asked.

I felt my left eyebrow creep up. "Like what kind of help?"

Lee hmphed. "Would you consider the job if I agreed to come manage the forestry part of the job?"

I shook my head. "Why don't you just do the job?"

"Because, I'm too damned old, and I want to be at least semi-retired. I don't know anything about protecting old-growth forest, but I sure as hell know how to minimize a forest fire. I know how to manage undergrowth and maximize the natural landscape to keep things moist and clear. I didn't want to influence you, though." He looked at Indigo, frustrated, but she smiled reassuringly. "Neither of us want to do a project this size alone, but I thought we could split the work between us and keep it manageable."

I uncrossed my arms, feeling less defensive now, but stared hard at my hands rather than meet Lee's expectant eyes.

"I'm willing to consider it, but Lee, I'll be upfront. I don't want to give up my art. If it's too overwhelming, I'd need to be able to step down from the job. Are you willing to take the project on if I try and it doesn't work out?"

I looked up to see Lee nodding in agreement. "I figured if it came to it, that would be your answer, and yes, for a while I could, but not long-term," he said. "I still want to travel with Indigo and see parts of the country I've never seen. I have grandbabies, too, that I want to spend more time with, but I also love Chemeketa, and Indigo and I both decided a long time ago that we'd retire here."

I sat silently thinking for a long time, and staring into the fire as the group chatted around me. When everyone began to break and head to their rooms, Lee stayed back with me. When we were alone, he said, "I intentionally dragged you here wanting you to spend some time in the forest. You know this area better than anyone else around. Even the locals don't know all the secret places like you do. Why don't you stay a few days, show that new man of yours around, and see if it feels right to you? If not, no harm, no foul, but if it does, consider my offer. I didn't mean for you to know about my partnership just yet. I wanted you to decide for yourself. I've already agreed to take over the interim position, so it doesn't make a difference whether you take it or not. Indigo and I are settled."

"Will you be moving up here?" I asked.

Lee smiled. "No, we've already prepurchased a town-home down in the retirement community. Ours will be backed up to the old forests and right off one of the old roads that winds its way up here. We're both ready to be less secluded, and want to be more involved with the Chemeketa community."

"So, this cabin would be mine?"

"Someone needs to live up here to keep an eye on the property, and make sure we catch any fires early enough to put them out."

Lee and I sat silently for several minutes, before I finally said, "I'll consider it, Lee, and yeah, I want to show Crea around. It would be good to be on neutral territory anyway."

Lee smiled, got up, and clapped me on the shoulder before saying goodnight and heading for bed.

I stayed where I was until I heard someone coming up behind me. I knew instantly it was Crea. The man seemed to make every nerve fiber in me sing when he was in my presence.

"You okay?" he asked as he sat next to me.

"I'm okay," I said, and sighed. "I knew it was coming, but didn't really know it at the same time. Does that make sense?"

Crea nodded. "Yeah, I guess I had the same thing going on with work, but, of course, I don't have the art to consider. It'd be a lot to give up, wouldn't it?"

"It could be, but I spend most of my time in the forests anyway." I chuckled. "Inspiration isn't an automatic thing for me. Before the leg incident, I'd walk through the woods, getting to know each of the trees until I began to envision a piece. I've spent over a year looking for inspiration before, so it isn't like I'm in my workshop twenty-four seven."

"So, is it possible you could wander around *these* woods until you get inspiration?"

I laughed. "These are the woods I usually wander around when I'm looking for inspiration. That's why I know them so well. This and Redwood National and State Parks in California."

"Have you been to Sequoia?" Crea asked.

"Of course. It's further away, though, so I prefer the forests I can get to in a day."

"Sounds sort of perfect then, huh?"

I just nodded. "Yeah, it sounds really perfect. Damn it!" I chuckled, and wrapped my arm around him. "Did you bring hiking boots?"

"Um, no," he said. "Why?"

"I have a proposal that requires a lot of hiking."

He looked at me strangely. "Go on."

"Would you like to spend some time navigating these forests with me while I try to figure out what I want to do?"

He didn't respond right away. "Is there a place to buy hiking boots close to here?" he finally asked, breaking the silence.

"Nope, that would require a trip to Portland or Salem."

He sighed. "Well, why the hell not. What about Jennie?"

I shook my head. "She needs to be back in the workshop. I've given her several things to practice, but I can ask her to stay if you want me to."

"No, I love her more than anything, but I'd like it to just be me and you."

I gave him a smile which might have been a little predatory, considering how many places I could imagine making love to him as the old trees stood guard.

"In that case, let's get up early and go to Portland, pick up supplies and buy you some hiking boots, and we can be back here by tomorrow afternoon."

It felt like something important had just happened, like the earth had shifted ever so slightly to fit into a better alignment.

We didn't make love that night. Instead, we lay in each other's arms, both of us clearly engrossed in our own thoughts.

CHAPTER SIXTEEN

CREA

BEFORE I KNEW IT, I was waking up to find we were still wrapped around each other.

Somehow, I moved out of his embrace without waking him and wandered down to the kitchen. This time, Indigo was standing at the coffee machine, just turning it on. I sat down at the counter to wait.

"So, are you staying with him?" she asked, and I nodded. "Good. However, I do have a warning. I dreamed about you two last night, and all the signs point to this being necessary, but not easy. You'll be tested while you're here. He will be forced to process his anger, and you'll be forced to deal with your abandonment."

I already knew that, or at least had the sense that something significant would take place here, but hearing Indigo confirm my suspicions made it feel more real and scarier.

She placed a cup of coffee in front of me. I figured my mind must have drifted since she'd somehow put the perfect amount of cream in it, and I hadn't even noticed her pouring the coffee, much less pulling the cream out of the refrigerator.

When I stared at the coffee, she laid her hand on mine.

"The thing about curses is they aren't fair. They're manifestations of other people's emotions cast upon us. Most of the time, anger, jealousy, frustration, envy... all the negative emotions that tend to hurt instead of heal. Emotions don't belong to others, though. They're ultimately the responsibility of the people who have them. I can't see it clearly, but I can feel the pain you've suffered with this one. Breaking that curse requires you to face the person who hurt you. Sometimes face to face, but most of the time, it's about facing your own emotions about that person. You've got a strong heart. I have no doubt you can overcome this. Just have faith in yourself and the person you're on this journey with. When two people work together in harmony, there isn't much they can't accomplish."

With that, she left me sitting alone in the kitchen. Within an hour, the three of them were headed out. Jennie had already decided she wanted to return with Lee and Indigo to get back to work on the skills Eli had taught her. I could tell he was proud of her for volunteering, and I couldn't help but feel more than a little proud of my niece myself.

When they were gone, we got in the shower together, since the hot water was almost gone. "If we had more hot water, I'd want to repeat the first shower we shared together," I told Eli, and he responded by pushing me up against the old pink tiles, and kissing me until all the blood left my brain and filled my cock.

He let me go, though, finished rinsing off, and stepped out of the shower to towel off.

I followed closely behind him, and asked, "What was that about?"

He smiled mischievously. "That, Crea, is a promise of *things to come*!" he said while waggling his eyebrows before he strode out of the room to get dressed.

Portland was where my grandma had gone to shop when she needed something Salem or McMinnville didn't have to offer. To be honest, I hadn't spent much time in the city since I left for college, but spending the day there shopping with Eli was a good way to give me a new perspective on the place.

Stopping at the shoe store first, Eli insisted on buying me hiking boots, but he wanted to pick the brand. When I protested, he asked how many more paychecks I had coming, and then told me he didn't want to be dealing with my blisters after he'd hiked me all over the countryside. In the end, he was acting so silly and funny he managed to pay without my knowing.

I demanded to pay for lunch and took him to a Southern-style restaurant known for its chicken and waffles that my grandmother used to love. He made me laugh until I cried tears as he named each of the chicken pieces like the characters in *Portlandia* did.

We shopped for food at Costco and got my favorite kielbasa at WinCo, then grabbed coffee at a small drive-thru coffee shop. I'd agreed to hand the car over to Eli since he knew where he was going. It was easier than him directing me or using the GPS on my phone, and when we left the city, he just kept driving. It was so natural to sit back and let him take control.

By the time we were headed back to Chemeketa, I'd seen an entirely different side of Eli and said as much.

"Most people think you're stoic and solemn. I read a lot about you before driving up to... well, to deal with the fallout, and there's no reference to your playful side."

Eli smiled at me and winked. "I don't go out in public often. When I do, it's almost always for business, and to be honest, it is pretty solemn for me when discussing business. Besides, I haven't found anyone who lets me just be me. Even when I went to college, my roommate was several years older and a bit of a prude. I hung out with a few people in the art department, but they were too much for me." He let his mind wander off for a moment before coming back. "I'm a bit of a loner. I guess that's why people see me as stoic."

"You aren't really. It appears you've enjoyed today as much as I have."

Eli reached over and grabbed my hand. "I *am* enjoying it as much as you, but that's because we have a connection."

I smiled because the thought that we had a connection warmed my heart in a goofy way. I looked at him with his adorable lopsided grin, and said, "I'm such a sap. Seriously, all you have to do is grin like that and I'm mush."

He lifted my hand and kissed it, causing my heart to do a little happy dance.

We were still in a great mood when we parked the car at the cabin. We were talking about something ridiculous and laughing as we approached the front door. We'd both missed the menacing mist that swirled around us and along the porch.

Eli noticed it first and put his arm across me, pulling me behind him. The second he did, my grandmother's ring began to burn uncomfortably hot against my skin, which hadn't happened before. Out of nowhere, a wolf appeared on the porch, but it was no normal wolf. This one was too big, too nasty, to be anything natural.

It snarled and snapped at us just like it was straight out of a horror movie. I stepped back around Eli, automatically reached into my pocket, and pulled out the amulet Indigo had given me. Tightly clutching it in my hand, I yelled, "You don't belong here!" Seconds after challenging the wolf to leave, it leaped at us, but disappeared before it landed a blow.

We stood where we were for a moment, catching our breath and letting our hearts calm down before moving. "Why is it always a fucking wolf?" I asked, breaking the tension.

"Huh?" Eli asked.

"Why is it these nasty things are always in the form of a wolf? Why not a bear or a mountain lion? As far as I know, we don't have wolves around here any longer."

I replaced the amulet in my pocket as Eli chuckled. "I'm not sure, maybe because that's what we fear, or because wolves are really scary?"

I shrugged. "Maybe. Oh well, it's gone now. You hungry?" I asked, and walked into the house, trying to sound braver than I felt.

Eli followed me in. "You know, it's probably going to get worse before it gets better."

I nodded. "I feel that too, and Indigo confirmed it this morning, but I'm not going to let my father's curse or his wolf-like cantation control me any longer, not if I can stop it."

"Your father's curse?"

"Yeah, my father cursed us when we came out to him. Me and my two brothers. He was pretending to be a Christian, so he could get elected to something he was running for, but that didn't stop him from using his powers to curse us."

"Fuck, that had to come back on him, though, in a bad way."

I shook my head. "I know my grandmother used to say things like that, but I don't know. I haven't seen him since, and I assume my brothers haven't either. That's his punishment, I guess. Well, and Lance cursed him back that he'd never have the love of his sons."

"Wow, who's Lance?"

"My older brother, Jennie's 'sperm daddy,' as she calls him."

Eli chuckled. "She mentioned him. You all have a strange family dynamic. You lived with your grandma in Chemeketa, correct?"

I nodded. "I wasn't here all that long before going off to college. Lance even less so, but our baby brother Kyle was here for a good portion of his childhood. You might have met him, Kyle Franklyn?"

Eli shook his head. "No, I was always a loner. My parents would come back to Chemeketa for the festivals, but I tended to disappear into the forests until they were over. I didn't know anyone who wasn't closely related to the trees."

The fear of seeing the wolf and feeling the threat it posed to us was beginning to pass. We put the groceries into the ancient refrigerator, and began prepping a picnic without even discussing that was what we were doing. After we were done, we found an old backpack and stuffed our food into it, along with a couple water bottles for each of us. Eli tossed it on his back, then knelt to help me lace up the new hiking boots.

"I've never owned a pair of these before," I confessed. "I like to hike well enough, but I don't think I've done enough to warrant whatever these cost."

Eli looked up and smiled. "You'll be glad you have them after we've walked a few of the routes I have planned, but we'll take it easy today until you've had a chance to wear them."

I liked the sound of that. I didn't really want to get a blister on my foot wearing in a new pair of boots, especially if he had plans for us to tour the entire forest while we were here.

Trekking anywhere from the cabin was straight down. The cliff went around the side and front of the cabin, but there was a tiny path that broke off from the end of the driveway and wound its way through the heavily wooded area and into the forests.

The moment we stepped onto the path, it was like being transported to a different dimension. The trees were *huge*, and their canopy hung over us. The birds chirped loudly, letting everyone who entered the area know it was their domain.

I should've been concerned about the mystical wolf that had attacked us earlier, but the forest felt so serene and protective, I didn't feel any danger.

As we walked, Eli pointed out different herbs that grew in the forest, and spoke about what each could be used for. I mostly just followed him, enjoying hearing him talk, and staring up into the magical canopy. The day was sunny, but I could tell we were in one of the misty forests the area was known for. I guessed there were a lot of days the mists owned the forest, and the thought caused a chill to run through me before I caught it, and pulled myself back by listening to Eli's rich, deep voice.

We'd walked what I'd guessed to be a little over a mile in an almost constant downward trek when we came to a stream running powerfully along a valley. Eli turned, and we walked upstream slowly enough that I was able to enjoy the change of temperature as well as the different bird and animal sounds. We came upon a rock wall, and I heard the waterfall before seeing it. Eli took me on a trail hidden by underbrush that wound its way through the rock on either side. When we emerged, it was into a large cavern. I recognized the place immediately from my dream and gasped. Eli must have thought the gasp was from the view, which was spectacular, but it was because the dream had been so vivid, and the lovemaking so amazing.

My cock filled at the memory, and when Eli finally turned to look at me, he immediately saw the lust in my expression.

He came to me, drew me into an embrace and kissed me like he had the first time I'd shown up at his cabin.

He pulled away just long enough to pull a blanket out of the backpack and spread it on the ground. Now that I saw the blanket, I recognized it from my dream, and wondered why I hadn't thought of that before when I saw Eli packing it.

We both lay down as we made out to the rhythm of the waterfall shielding the entrance to the cave.

It was chilly, but Eli's body next to mine kept me warm. When I felt something against my back, I reached around and pulled out the amulet. Eli looked down and asked what it was.

I laughed. "Indigo gave it to me as a protection stone, I think." I then held up my hand to show Eli the ring. "This belonged to my grandma. They're both emeralds, although this one is rough stone." I showed him the amulet again.

He took it from me, and an electric shock passed through both of us. "I think that might belong more to you than me," I said.

He looked at the amulet and smiled. "It's so ancient-looking," he said with wonder as he fingered the amulet. "I'm guessing this is English hawthorn."

I was perplexed, and asked, "How can you tell?"

"Just a feeling."

He handed it back and leaned over to kiss me. "You know what hawthorn represented to the druids?"

I smiled. "I'm guessing by the look on your face it's something to do with sex."

"Male sexuality, to be precise," he said. "It supposedly makes you horny."

"The original woody?" I said, chuckling.

He crawled on top of me, pressing his body into mine. "I'd say it's working."

"Good," I said, and began to grind my clothed cock into his.

I rolled over on my side, placing the amulet on a small ledge just above us before we took each other.

After making love more passionately than even my dream, I reached for the amulet again. "You should keep this. Maybe it can be more useful than just to make us both horny. I'm guessing we're both plenty horny without it."

He chuckled, taking the amulet from me, and twisting it around, looking at the intricacy. "It's also supposed to be a protective wood. Hawthorn is known for love and marriage, and for protection and sex. It's one of my favorite English woods."

I lay back, staring at the ceiling of the cave. "Wonder why Indigo didn't give it to you herself."

He leaned over and kissed my nipple, then used his tongue to stimulate it before saying, "Probably because you were supposed to give it to me."

I leaned up on my side and took his mouth with mine. "Is it strange that even after just meeting you, I have all these feelings swirling around inside me?"

"If it helps, I do too."

"Do you think it's just this fucked-up curse shit?" I asked.

"I think the curse would be doing the opposite. Think more, big bad wolf waiting for you on the front porch."

I nodded. "But don't you think this is a little like being manipulated?"

He shrugged and lay back down. "I think we're definitely being led a certain way, and I had dreams about you before I even knew you. But I know enough about how magic works to know you get to choose, or rather, *have* to choose your own destiny. Magic doesn't have the power to force a person to do something they don't want to, but it can push you in a certain direction."

"It doesn't bother you? Being pushed?" I asked.

He shook his head. "Not as long as I know once the ride is over, I can get off if I want to."

I lay back, but didn't curl into him as I would've before the conversation.

"I've had terrible relationships. I tend to attract horrible men who are mean and hateful."

"Did they hurt you?" he asked, sitting up so he could look at me.

"Never physically, but they did hurt my heart in every way possible. My father's curse was that I could never be loved by a man. It didn't, however, prevent me from loving the wrong man."

Eli lay back down. "Some of us have made bad choices without having had a curse on us."

"That's true, but at least you had a choice."

"So do you," Eli said. "Curses are like anything else. They require your compliance to work. That's why I'm guessing the wolf came to visit. You aren't being compliant any longer."

"I suppose so. You make it sound so cut and dried, but it has never felt like my choice. Bad men came, and I let them in. I guess it's just easier to think I didn't have any control over it."

"Confession?" Eli said, and looked over at me. I nodded, and he continued. "I avoided relationships, not because I'm cursed, but because I'm a coward, well, maybe mostly because I'm selfish. I haven't wanted to share my life, thinking I wanted it all to myself. Curse, magic, or whatever, you're the first person I've considered letting in this far."

"That's scary, dude, you're putting your eggs in the wrong basket. You should seriously reconsider!"

Eli laughed and put the amulet on my chest. Both the amulet and my ring immediately warmed against my skin. He slid his hand down and cupped my ass. "I think this is the perfect basket for my eggs."

Chapter Seventeen

Eli

WE HIKED BACK UP the mountain. I wanted to see how much Crea could handle before taking him on a longer, more strenuous hike, and I knew climbing back up to the cabin was the best indication of that.

He laughed and flirted all the way back, not even commenting on the strenuous climb. When we got back to the cabin, he only hesitated a moment, moving his hand that held his grandmother's ring in front of him, apparently looking for any more signs of wolf-laced fog. Seeing none, he continued his chipper conversation into the cabin.

He collapsed onto the uncomfortable nineteen sixties chair, still covered in plastic that made it feel even worse, and looked around. "So, if you stay, are you going to redecorate?" he asked.

I laughed out loud from my place in the kitchen, and said, "Without a doubt!"

"What would you do?" he asked.

I went over to him and began untying his laces and removing his boots. That must have done something to him, because his expression went from inquisitive to hungry. I was beginning to get good at recognizing that look.

I ignored it for the moment and looked around. "Besides getting rid of all this horrible furniture, I'd want to vault the ceiling in this part of the house, maybe putting a larger window to enjoy the views toward the ocean."

"Wouldn't that be expensive?" he asked as he looked toward the area I was talking about.

"Yeah, if you don't know how to do it yourself."

He smiled. "And you do?"

"And I do."

"What else would you do?" he asked.

"I'd redo the kitchen, but not in modern granite or marble. Instead, I'd use natural wood from the forest to redo the old sixties plywood cabinets, and put down a live edge from the old-growth trees for the countertops and island."

"That sounds beautiful," he said, and stood up to walk through the kitchen. "I'd redo the layout in here, so it looks out through the big window you're creating. Make it flow. More feng shui."

"My gods, you've been in California too long."

He laughed. "It's a thing, trust me. I can tell when energy is flowing or stuck, and it is definitely stuck in here."

"Tell me how you'd do it," I said, indulging him.

We talked for about an hour about how to design the kitchen using natural wood, but also using some of my art techniques to enhance it, so it didn't just look like a blob of wood on top of more wood.

By the time we got to bed, we both collapsed before we could do much more than simply make out.

We were back on the hill where I'd gotten hurt. Stumps surrounded us. Crea sat on a stump facing me, and asked, "So, are we in the dream together this time?"

"Well, maybe. I can see you, if that's what you're asking."

He came over and leaned into me. "You feel pretty real."

I leaned down and kissed him, and heard a familiar voice behind us say, "Guys, get a room."

We turned, and the funny little woman that had plagued the dreams stood before us.

"Hi, Grandma," Crea said.

I looked at him and asked, "This is your grandma?"

He nodded. "Grandma, meet Eli. Eli, meet my grandma, Gwen."

"We've met," she said, smiling.

She turned toward the woods and frowned. "You need to be prepared. Things will get more dangerous. Keep your protections around you." Both the ring and the amulet that appeared in my hand glowed momentarily. "With these, you can find each other, but"—she looked at Crea—"he will fight you with all his strength."

She looked sad for a moment and shook her head, saying, "Crea, he can't help it, what's put in motion can't be reversed. Not until you overcome it and push the hatred away."

Crea nodded. "We know, Grandma."

She reached out and touched his hand. "I love you, Crea. Be brave and be strong."

She reached out with her other hand and touched mine, saying, "Take care of him."

I woke up and went to the bathroom. I'd gotten so used to the dreams now, I didn't even think it was that unusual. I was just curious if that was indeed his grandma I'd been seeing.

When I came back into the bedroom, Crea was sitting up in bed. "Did you have the same dream?"

I shrugged. "It depends. Was it on the top of a hill with stumps all around, and was an old woman there in tie-dye clothes?" He nodded. "Well, so I know who she is now, that's cool."

"I guess," he said. "It's difficult seeing her, knowing she's gone and..."

I sat down beside him. "And?"

"Well, I was so resistant to coming back to Chemeketa, I hadn't seen her as much as I'd wanted to."

"You're seeing her now. I can tell she loves you a lot. And, she's not technically gone if she's able to visit you and me in our dreams."

"Maybe," Crea said.

I pulled him into my arms and lay back down, spooning him from behind.

"I was so sad when my parents died. They were such a huge part of my life. Mom died first, and then a year later my dad died, I think from a broken heart. It's like losing a part of your soul."

Crea nodded and said, "I didn't really miss my dad after we moved in with my grandma, I assumed because of the counter curse, but it hurt every day my mom rejected us. She never came to check on us, not even once. I heard through Grandma that she and Dad had divorced, and she'd gone to live in Texas. My brother,

Kyle, said she's living back in Salem now with her parents. I don't know anything about her other than that."

I held him tight as he let the memories flow through him.

"Parents can be really hateful. It feels like your grandma loved you, though."

I could feel him smile. "She was always like liquid sunshine. She was upbeat and brought such happiness to us even though we were so... broken. I think it was harder on my brother Lance, because he was gone shortly after all that went down with Dad. He didn't get to bask in her sunshine quite as long as we did."

I held him as he quieted and eventually fell asleep again. I didn't want to wake him, but I was wired after the dream. If I were by myself, I'd pack up and disappear into the woods for a while, but I figured he needed me for now, so I lay next to him, comforting him until I finally fell asleep myself.

A phone started ringing early the next morning. Both of us tried to ignore it, but it rang and rang until we both got up to find where the damned thing was.

Finally, Crea found it outside the bedroom and down the hall. It was hidden in a cabinet, another nineteen sixties thing. He answered the phone, the likes of which I hadn't seen since the nineteen nineties.

"Hello?"

I could hear the tinny voice on the other end as I leaned up against the wall next to him.

"Hello, boys, I wondered if you were going to just ignore the call or if you'd answer."

"Donna, it's sort of early, wouldn't you say?" Crea asked.

"Honey," I could hear her chuckling. "It's after ten. I'm an old hippie, and I get up earlier than that."

He looked at his watch and sighed. "Sorry, I didn't realize."

"Well, no problem. So I can be by in an hour to pick you up for our lunch with the Earth Guild."

"Oh, Donna, I'd forgotten all about that. Hold on just a moment," he said, then looked at me. "Do you have plans for me today, or is it okay for me to go with them?"

"No plans from me, go and enjoy. I'd like to spend some time alone in the forest anyway, just to get my head on straight about the job offer."

He nodded and put the phone back up to his ear. "Donna, that sounds fine. So, you'll be here around eleven then?"

I heard her confirm it, and they hung up.

"Well, so much for morning sex. I feel thwarted," he said, but chuckled.

"I'll make it up to you later, I promise."

Crea smiled. "I'd better get ready."

"I'll make coffee," I said as I started down the old shag carpeted stairs.

We were sitting at the Formica-covered table sipping our coffees when Donna arrived. I went to let her in, and Crea downed his cup and rushed up the stairs.

"Sorry, Donna, we lost track of time. Let me brush my teeth and I'll be ready."

She smiled at me as he rushed off, and said, "So, that's going well, I see."

I smiled back at her. "Well, it was until some busybody called us and woke us up before our morning sex session."

"Busybody, my ass. You need to do like the rest of us and wake up earlier, so you can get your morning sex session in."

I just hmphed cheerfully and put my arm around her. "Want a cup of coffee?"

"Nah, I'm caffeinated to the hilt. I went to visit my friend Josephine this morning at her bakery. You know she roasts her own beans there now."

I barely knew who Josephine was, and had only picked up a pastry there once or twice when I'd rushed up from home and hadn't come prepared to spend time in the forests. Sometimes I'd spend several days there, and even pastry that had gone stale was better than going hungry.

Crea came down, gave me a minty-fresh peck on the mouth, and followed Donna out the door. The moment he was gone, it felt empty and dark in the cabin, like someone had doused a fire and turned the lights off.

No longer wanting to be in the cabin by myself, I got dressed, left a message for Crea telling him it'd be gone a while for my hike but back before dark, and walked into the woods. I knew of a hidden trail I suspected even Old Man Ellefson didn't know about that went into the deeper part of the woods, a part that was magically blocked from view.

When the Natives lost their lands because of the forest fire in the late eighteen hundreds, a small tribe, who'd lost most of their members, ended up on this ridge. They were here when our community began to inhabit the area, but instead of the manifest destiny shit that was destroying tribes in the rest of the country, the people

who settled in Chemeketa embraced the small indigenous population.

The two groups eventually mingled and intermarried.
Using their mixed heritage of magic from the Euro-
pean settlers and the traditional tribal medicine of the
indigenous people, they warded a large section of the
old-growth forest that had been used as a holy place
long before the settlers arrived.

The people named this part of the forest Kelim, although it was a much larger area before the great fire
took place. Over the years, the name had been short-
ened to Kels.

For some reason, the wards never worked on me. I
could feel them and knew they were there, but they
didn't confuse me or push me away like they did to other
hikers. Instead, the forests here seemed to welcome me,
even embrace me. Supposedly, my ancestors had been
some of the original Kels, but that was many generations
back.

So, I'd come to know the holy people who still occupied these woods, although not full-time like my ancestors did.

One of my best friends since childhood was Edward
Edenfield. He and I met in the forest when we were
young, and during one of my many days spent exploring,
we became immediate friends. Since Ed's father had
passed away, he'd become the unofficial leader of the
Kels. I seldom went far on the trail in this part of the
forest before Ed met me. He always knew I was coming,
and today was no exception.

He stepped in front of me and grabbed me, tossing me
onto the ground, then yelled a crazy war cry reminiscent

of what he did the first time he found me wandering along the secret trails into this part of the forest.

"You know I'm getting too old for you to keep tossing me around like this." I chuckled as I picked myself off the ground.

"Whatever," he said, smiling, then reached down a hand to help me up. "I did hear about your accident. How's the leg?"

"Healing well, except when random Kel men toss me around like a bag of potatoes."

He pulled me into a bear hug, and chuckled. "Come on, Lydia is with me. We felt you enter the forest and assumed you'd come to see us."

I followed behind the man, framed as big as me but significantly stronger, into the old village down by the mountain stream, which ran into the larger one that made the waterfall where Crea and I had made love yesterday.

Lydia was a short, dark-skinned woman who'd met and fallen madly in love with Ed about twenty years ago. Her mom was from Che, but her dad was from northern Arizona. Like me, she'd been naturally attracted to the forest, and had met Ed while out exploring. They fell in love as instantly as my friendship with Ed had developed, and got married several years ago. Now she worked alongside him when they were called to provide care to the people who preferred a more traditional form of medicine than doctors and drugs.

Lydia greeted me with a hug when we walked into the old-fashioned log structure next to the stream.

It was built around a century and a half ago and was still used today, but more for ceremonies and the occasional meeting of the Kels.

When I walked into the longhouse, I saw a big fire in the middle of the open space. Usually, at this time of year, they kept the fires lower. There were several things surrounding the fire I'd never seen before. I was welcome in the village, but I'd never actually been allowed to witness their rituals or ceremonies.

I looked questioningly at Ed, and he smiled a hesitant smile.

Lydia took my hand, and said, "You are being faced with a darkness, one that grows in anger. That anger is living inside you, and we felt it when you first entered the forest. You must cleanse yourself and ask the guardian spirits of your ancestors to help you repel it."

I wasn't surprised Lydia and Ed had figured out I was dealing with something. I was surprised they were volunteering to help. It was my understanding you had to ask the medicine men and women for help. When I mentioned it to Ed later, he shrugged. "I'm your brother, that makes this different."

Lydia led me to the fire, and asked me to strip down to my underwear. Had anyone else asked me to do that, I'd have flat-out refused, but working with Ed and Lydia was the same or even better than seeing a nurse or doctor.

She handed me a wooden chalice and asked me to drink. It tasted fresh like spring water, which I assumed it was, then she rubbed my chest with what smelled like tallow with a mixture of herbs, and chanted words I didn't understand. When she was done, she left the building, and I didn't see her again. Ed asked me to follow him, taking me to where the stream met the larger creek. "You'll have to go barefoot," he said. "You can't have modern footwear interrupting your bathing."

I had tender feet, so it took a while to get into the stream. Finally, he instructed me to strip the rest of the way, and bathe every part of my body in the cold water, paying special attention to the insides of my ears and other crevices. "You must completely cover your body with the healing waters, until you feel especially clean."

The water was really cold. I'd bathed in streams before, but damn, only in midsummer, not this early in the year. I shivered while I did as he asked, moving as quickly as I could.

Ed sat on the bank of the creek, chanting or moving around where I'd entered the water. After a few seconds, I tried to leave, and Ed just laughed at me and shook his head. "Not quite yet, my friend. You've got to cleanse your entire body for this to work."

I sighed and almost flipped him the bird, but decided against it, considering this was supposed to be a holy ceremony.

Finally, after I thought I was going to freeze my nuts off, Ed stood and motioned me toward him. He wrapped me with an old blanket. I was all too glad of it, considering I was shivering.

I gingerly followed Ed back to the longhouse. When we arrived, Ed sat me in front of the fire and lit a smudge stick. When he blew it out, the smoke surrounded me. He used a seagull's feather to direct the smoke and continued his chants. I felt the drowsiness instantly, and there was little I could do to stop it.

I didn't know how long I slept, but when I woke, neither Ed nor Lydia were anywhere to be seen. The fire was just a pile of cold ashes, so I assumed I'd been out for several hours.

I found my clothes perfectly folded and sitting just inside and to the right of the door, and got dressed. When I stepped outside, the cantation in the form of a wolf stood on the village boundary, staring at me. The mist swirled around it, but it neither moved nor made a sound.

There were spirits all around me that I hadn't noticed at first because they looked more like the mist than people.

The wolf was clearly afraid of the spirits who all began to converge upon him. The wolf turned and bounded up the mountain into the trees before he stopped and gave me one last menacing look before leaping up and out of sight.

The mists continued to swirl around me, and I could feel a strong sense of peace.

I hiked back through the woods in what felt like a dream. At times, I felt as if I were one of the spirits dancing in the mists, and at other times, I felt solid and human again. I wondered what Lydia had put in the drink she'd given me. Whatever it was, she could make a killing on the black market.

I think the spirits might've left me when I entered the cabin, but I was still too drugged to notice. I crossed to the old sofa and lay down on it before passing out again.

Chapter Eighteen

CREA

DONNA WAS CHIPPER AS we drove down the mountain and out of the old-growth forests. She had a hundred questions about what I'd done in San Francisco and about modern gardening techniques.

"I'm a huge fan of square-foot gardening, especially in small spaces. It wasn't unusual for us to harvest over a hundred pounds of tomatoes out of an eight-by-four-foot area. We also grew marigolds and basil among that crop. Square-foot gardening is the best way to incorporate companion planting," I said in response to her questions.

I explained several different techniques, including hay bales and layering, before we stepped out of her truck and into the beautiful old Craftsman-style home of Mr. Henry.

The place was buzzing when we walked in. Of course, there were older people like those who ran the council, but I was also pleased to see people my age and even younger in the mix.

Donna introduced me to everyone as we walked through the group, but the names just whirled through my head and out my ears. Finally, I met Jack Henry, who owned the home, and I commented on how beautiful it was. The old man smiled, but sadness filled his eyes.

Later, Donna whispered that the home belonged to Jack's husband's family. Jack had taken the Henry name when he and Fred had their handfasting ceremony back in the seventies.

I recognized a couple of the people from my childhood, although I couldn't remember their names. Thankfully, they introduced themselves and saved me the embarrassment.

We finally sat down at tables that were set up around the room. There were homemade yeast rolls, cold cuts, homemade pickles, and a variety of other foods spread out on each table, and everyone helped themselves.

I made a sandwich with one of the rolls, and when I bit into it, I thought I was going to drool. When I swallowed, I leaned over to Donna, and admitted it was the best roll I'd ever tasted.

"I told you so," she said. "That old man can cook!"

After we'd all eaten, everyone talked at once, and Donna finally stood up, drawing attention to herself.

"Thank you, Jack, for allowing us to meet here again and, of course, for your homemade rolls." The group clapped and cheered the old man, who blushed sweetly.

"The main agenda for today is the new gardens surrounding the Grange House. Like me, there are a lot of us older folks who no longer have the energy to plow the fields like we used to, and there are plenty of younger families wanting and needing housing in the area. Many of us are going to sell our homes to these younger folks, with the hope of preserving our community and the traditions that have been part of our heritage for over a century and a half."

I could tell a lot of this was for my benefit, so I listened carefully as she reviewed the last meeting's talking points.

"We may be old, but we still value fresh vegetables, so giving up our gardens is the hardest part of moving into senior living. That's why we've come up with the idea of converting the Grange House lands into a large vegetable garden. The council has asked us to be in charge of that. So, before we go any further, let's open the discussion on the particulars of the gardens."

The conversation was a typical Roberts Rules of Order format in that there were motions, then they'd forget there were motions, then Donna got frustrated and told people to pull their thumbs out of their asses and just talk normally.

After about thirty minutes, Jack passed around another tray of hot rolls, which shut down most of the conversation long enough for Donna to call for a vote. It was unanimous. Everyone wanted the gardens, especially since the council had agreed to pay a significant amount to set them up, and ensure there was someone to supervise the whole enterprise.

"We will also be in charge of hiring someone to manage the gardens. That deserves another conversation, but for the sake of the gods, let's not do the damned motion thing again," Donna said with frustration.

There was much less discussion on the new topic. No one wanted the job, even though it paid really well. I noticed the younger people in the crowd were trying to look small as they sat in their uncomfortable folding chairs, and that almost made me laugh.

Finally, when the conversation came to a natural and uncomfortable lull, Donna announced that I'd worked in San Francisco as an urban agriculture organizer. Of course, the entire group sat up and took notice, and I gave Donna a nasty look, causing her to almost spit out her tea.

Donna recovered, and asked me to give the group some pointers on what we needed to look for in a manager.

I stood after I gave Donna another nasty look, and began with some of the things I thought they needed to consider.

"Thanks, it's an honor to hang out with you all today, and Mr. Henry, those rolls are so good, I've had to bite my tongue several times to keep myself from asking you to marry me."

The group laughed, and several people nodded.

"You have a pretty significant task ahead of you. Managing a farm by committee is very different from plowing up your own farm and planting what you want." I chuckled as I thought about how disdainful Eli had been about running the forest by committee.

There were several nods, which made it easier for me to continue.

"You'll also have to decide what method you're going to use on the farm. Will you be setting up plots, or making a set of gardens like they do on regular farms? Are you going to be organic, or allow commercial fertilizers and pesticides to be used?"

I almost laughed out loud at the hiss that went around the room when I mentioned fertilizers and pesticides.

"My strongest advice is that you find someone you trust and let them run the farm, and don't micromanage them too much. Remember, no matter what they're paid, they will be doing the job of three or four people. That's just how farming is, and the more you force your farm manager to deal with petty or even valid concerns, the less time they'll be managing volunteers or working the soil."

Glancing around, I saw confirmation that I'd been heard, so I thanked them again and sat down.

Donna stood back up, and asked, "All those in favor of hiring Mr. Franklyn say aye."

I gaped at her as the room echoed a resounding, "Aye!"

"The ayes have it," Donna said, without asking for the nays.

I stood back up before anything else could be said and thanked them again. "It's a wonderful offer, but I live in San Francisco. I can't accept a position here."

Disappointed faces surrounded me, and Donna patted my back. "Well dear, we've already voted, so when you come to your senses, just let me know."

Then she basically pushed me back into my seat and continued the meeting. When it was over, several people came up to congratulate me on the position, and told me how much they looked forward to my getting on with the project. I pasted a smile on my face, and thought about the different ways I could dispose of Donna's body. I could almost hear my grandmother giggling at my expense.

Donna laughed all the way back to the cabin. My arguments and frustration just amused her more. "You are just like her," I finally said. Donna looked over with a sweet smile on her face.

"That's a wonderful thing to say. She'd want you to come home."

"Donna, my life is in San Francisco. I don't even have a place to live here."

We were just coming up on the cabin when she said, "Looks like a nice enough place to me." I squinted at her, but something had caught her attention. "Kels," she said under her breath.

I looked out, and mist was sweeping around the home. It was different from the last mist. It didn't seem sinister like the wolf's did.

She shook her head. "I can tell your grandmother has a hand in this," she said. "But, be careful. Spirits have their own agendas, and it's not always the agenda you have."

"Sort of like going to a luncheon and having a group you just met vote to give you a job you didn't apply for?"

"You'll thank me when you come to your senses," she said. "And it's easier to get the vote out of the way now, so you can start when you're ready."

I leaned over and kissed her cheek. "You're still just as ornery as you ever were," I said.

She winked and said, "Oh no, I'm much worse now."

I waved at her as she drove off and walked through the playful, dry mist to the cabin door.

When I walked in, I saw two things. First, there was a fire in the grate, and smoke was moving around the room, not unlike the mist outside. Second, Eli's huge frame was lying prostrate on the old sofa, most of his body hanging off it.

The smoke didn't smell like smoke, so I knew this was whatever Donna had called the Kels. Since I didn't detect anything negative from the spirits, I left him alone on the sofa and went into the kitchen to put together dinner.

I'd managed to snag a handful of Jack's delicious rolls, which I intended to use tonight to romance Eli through his stomach. I wasn't a particularly good cook, although I loved fresh veggies and fruits. Mostly, I spent my time canning or preserving food, not necessarily cooking it.

Despite that, we had a nice assortment of cheese, a nice pork roast, and makings for various other dishes.

I pulled the pork roast out, put it into a Tupperware container I found tucked neatly beside the stove, and marinated it with lemon juice from the refrigerator. I also found some spices that weren't out of date, and luckily found what I needed to make a rub a Cuban friend of mine taught me that tasted remarkable on pork. After coating and covering the meat, I stuck it into the refrigerator.

I cut up some potatoes, carrots, and a rutabaga we'd bought in Portland and covered them with a kitchen towel that I'd found folded neatly in one of the drawers. Not for the first time, I wondered what kind of straight man managed such an immaculate home?

Eli was still out cold when I'd finished preparing dinner, so I went upstairs and collapsed onto the bed for my own nap. Eli woke me up not much later, kissing me on the neck, and grinding his delicious body into mine.

CHAPTER NINETEEN

ELI

I'D WOKEN UP RAVENOUSLY horny, and immediately went upstairs to find Crea. I didn't know how I knew he was there, I just did, and my hunger for him was so all-consuming, I felt as if I were being dragged to him.

After he drained me, I was still hungry for him. I hadn't come that much since my twenties, and I knew it was likely thanks to the stuff Lydia had given me. Crea didn't seem to mind though, and I had to remind myself to find out what it was she'd given me, since a man of my age needed to keep stamina medication at his disposal at all times.

Crea all but hummed with pleasure next to me. I chuckled, knowing I could probably fuck him again, but he looked so gloriously worn out, I didn't have it in me to take him again so soon.

I pulled Crea into the shower, and just enjoyed running my hands and cock over his body as I cleaned him and myself up from our powerful sex session.

He dried off and went downstairs still naked, saying he needed to finish making dinner. I was having a hard time keeping my dick out of him, and watching him cook in the buff wasn't going to help my libido calm down any, so I decided to lie on the bed and cool off for a moment.

Thoughts of the day swirled through my head. In particular, the spirits that had flowed around me as I walked up to the cabin from the Kel village. That was when it struck me. "Fuck," I said out loud. "I was possessed, no wonder I had all this stamina."

I chuckled. I would be kicking a certain shaman's ass when I saw him again. Still, no harm, no foul, and I fully intended to take advantage of the possession for the length of time it lasted. My understanding was it didn't usually take long before one spirit took guardianship and forced the others to leave.

I managed to keep it together long enough to eat the meal Crea cooked and make a fire for us to sit by. However, by the time Crea sat next to me, the smell of his skin intoxicated me, and I couldn't keep my hands off him.

When we did manage to get back upstairs, I collapsed onto the big bed, and despite having slept most of the day, I fell into a deep sleep.

CHAPTER TWENTY

CREA

THE FOG HUNG ON the windows as Eli slept next to me. I'd felt their presence for as long as I'd been back from the lunch with Donna. Eli had been sexually ravenous, and I knew that was as much about whatever these mists were as it was his desire for me. Still, I was as sexually attracted to him as I could be, and although the sex might be less about who he was and more about whatever spell was cast, I enjoyed it while it lasted. Besides, the mists didn't feel particularly dangerous, although they were far from benign.

Not being able to sleep, I slipped back downstairs and began cleaning the dinner dishes. The place didn't have a dishwasher, which wasn't really a surprise considering its age, so I hand-washed and dried them, then put them away.

It was well after midnight by the time I finally got done. When I went back up to the bedroom, Eli was sprawled across the bed. I chuckled at the sight. I could either wake him up or just sleep in one of the other bedrooms.

I decided to sleep in another room, taking the one I'd stayed in the night we first arrived. It took a while to fall asleep, the day's events circling in my head. I wondered if I could be happy being in Chemeketa again after all these years.

If I were honest with myself, I'd stayed away because of the memories of being abandoned by my parents. Coming to Chemeketa had been so devastating. So much had been lost that it overshadowed the happy thoughts that went along with living with the unconditional love of my grandmother.

Donna had brought back many of those memories today, and while sitting among the Earth Guild members, I'd felt like I belonged. And another honest admission... it felt more like home than any place I'd lived in the past twenty-five years.

I could see myself living here even after Eli and I eventually broke up, which, of course, we would. We were in a bubble, a moment out of time, and I needed to remember it wouldn't last, no matter how much that thought hurt. Even if it was living alone like Mr. Ellefson had for all those years in this huge cabin, or how Mr. Henry was living now without his husband but surrounded by friends, I could create a content enough life here.

By the time I fell asleep, I had almost convinced myself this was where I wanted to move. I even thought I might call Donna tomorrow and let her know.

The mists swarmed around me. I was in the fields by the Grange House. Every place the mists touched caught fire. People I couldn't see screamed in the background, and I knew it was the citizens of Chemeketa.

Fire burned through the old-growth forests, and I was instantly transported to the cabin, which blazed. I looked inside the window and saw Eli sprawled out on the old sofa like he had been earlier in the day. The fire blazed around him, but he didn't move.

"If you stay, you will destroy everything here."

The voice was Donna's. She stood across from me, dressed in black, and I could see she embodied the wolf. "You are cursed, and everything you touch is cursed. Everything will die and burn because of you."

I screamed as the flames began to engulf the sofa and Eli, but I couldn't move, couldn't get to him.

Donna's laughter chilled me. "I will never let you go," she said, and when I turned around, Donna had turned back into the wolf. "I am your companion, I am your lover. Anything or anyone you love will be destroyed, and you will be the person to blame."

"Go away!" I screamed at the animal. "Save him!"

I didn't know which command I wanted the wolf to follow, both maybe.

"You can save him, but you must leave now, leave before I force this to end."

I woke with a start, unable to catch my breath. I automatically reached with my thumb to touch the ring and noticed then that it was gone. Somehow it had disappeared. I searched frantically through the bed and then down the stairs and around the living room.

When I didn't find it, I rushed to the bedroom where Eli was still asleep and searched through the bathroom, sure I'd lost it when we'd showered. Finally, not seeing it, I woke Eli and searched the bed.

"Crea, what's wrong?" he asked.

"I can't find it. I can't find the ring!"

He moved off the bed and tried to console me, but I pushed him away and searched the now empty bed.

It was nowhere to be seen. I'd lost my protection, Eli's protection. I was useless!

The thoughts I'd worked hard to ignore since my childhood came pouring back. I was a plague. My father had turned me so that everyone I touched turned to ashes. The fire was more than just a metaphor. It was real. I'd lost my family when I'd moved, and now I'd lost my job.

I was in a panic, and the more Eli tried to calm me, the more I freaked out.

"I have to leave!" I finally said. I looked at Eli and shook my head. "I have to leave. I can't stay here, I'm putting all of you at risk."

"Shh, Crea, take a deep breath and tell me what happened."

I tried to do as he asked. I sat on the bed, and although I knew I was close to a panic attack, I told him my dream, how I'd been the reason the forest was on fire. I cried as I told him I couldn't move as the fire engulfed him.

"You'll die if I stay," I said, convinced it was true. "My only hope was the ring, that fucking ring that I've lost!"

"Crea, it was just trying to scare you. You have to fight it. I'm here with you."

"No, Eli, you aren't… this isn't real. You and I have been riding some fantasy, a magical spell. I've been in and out of relationships since I was old enough to date. They don't ever work out, they don't ever succeed. You'll get tired of me and turn nasty, just like all the others."

Eli tried to comfort me again, but I jumped up.

"I'm sorry, I have a life in California. I have to get back to civilization. I need to find a job," I said as I began fumbling through clothes and stuff I'd taken out of my bag. I tossed clean and dirty clothes on top of each other as I packed my stuff.

I zipped my bag and rushed down the stairs, Eli trying to talk me down, but I knew... I knew if I didn't go now, I might stay and put everyone in danger. I wasn't willing to do that, not for the chance of love. Maybe if it was a sure thing, I'd try, but experience told me it would fail, and in the end, the curse would consume him and Chemeketa.

I rushed around the cabin, making sure I'd packed everything, then headed to the car. Eli watched, but I couldn't look him in the face. I knew I'd see hurt and confusion there, and I also knew it was how things had to be.

I left him standing in the doorway, his silhouette against the light all I could see as I drove the winding pothole-filled road back down the mountain and through the woods.

Before I made it out of the forest, I saw the wolf that transformed into my dad's cantation standing on the edge of the road watching me as I drove past. His glee was evident, and I could feel it in my entire being. It didn't matter, I knew it was right. I couldn't beat this. I had to accept it and live with it. The only thing I had the power to do was keep it from destroying the people I cared about.

That realization struck me in the heart. Eli was the first and only lover I'd ever felt this much for. The only potential mate I might have loved. For that reason, I'd leave and stay gone. For that reason, I'd run. I'd save him even if it meant I'd never save myself.

Chapter Twenty-One

Eli

THE GUARDIAN SPIRITS HAD been strong. I'd been drugged with their possession, but by the time I was woken up by Crea, the intensity had begun to wane. I'd known even before he woke me something was wrong. I could feel the darkness as it poured into the cabin, slipping around the edges as the guardian spirits began to dissipate.

Crea was inconsolable. I'd tried touching him, talking to him, but nothing helped. I was helpless as he packed and rushed out the door and out of my life. I left messages on his phone, knowing there was no coverage once you left the hilltop, but I had to try.

Finally, I fell on the living room sofa, his loss weighing heavily upon me.

I reached down and felt the amulet in my pocket, and wondered if maybe I should've had him keep it. Maybe it would've helped to keep the nightmare that had scared him at bay.

Maybe if I hadn't been such a fucking horndog, he'd have been able to confide in me. Maybe if I hadn't been possessed, I could've had him in my arms and known when he was afraid... maybe, maybe, maybe... I knew I had to stop that line of thought. It wasn't helpful.

I needed to think logically. What did he need? What would help?

The ring, he'd been looking for the ring. So, I decided I'd start there, then I'd rally the troops. He might be running, but there were things we could do on this end.

Indigo and Lee sat across the nineteen fifties linoleum table from Donna and Jennie as I paced up and down the length of the kitchen.

Donna shook her head. "I know you're frustrated, Eli, but Crea and his brothers have been through so much. When their dad cursed them, they were tossed out like garbage. Even their mom abandoned them. If it wasn't for their grandmother, bless her soul, they'd have been thrust into foster care."

I continued pacing restlessly. Ever since the night Crea had told me how he'd redo the kitchen, I'd seen this part of the house as a part of him. Being close to it felt like I was close to him.

Indigo watched me much as she would've watched a caged animal, with both pity and anxiety.

"How do we help him?" I asked.

Indigo said, "Honey, he has to find his own way. The curse has him now. It grows stronger with his fear, his giving in."

"Why didn't anyone tell him that?" I yelled across the room.

Lee stood up and pulled me into a hug. "We did, son, as much as we could."

I broke down as Lee's fatherly embrace engulfed me. "There must be something we can do."

Indigo came and stood beside us. "There may be, but I don't think the two of you had enough time. He'd have to be connected with you on a deep emotional level for anything to work."

"Well, I'm attached to him, doesn't that count?" I asked, imploring her.

"Of course, it does, but to reach him, he has to have the same feelings."

"Let's try. The least we can do is try, right?"

I could hear the desperation in my voice. I'd been devastated and worried since he left. I called Indigo and Lee early the next morning, and they grabbed Jennie and came over right away. Indigo must have called Donna, because she arrived right after them. I didn't ask how she knew. I was too worried about Crea to ask.

Jennie hadn't spoken. The worry on her face matched the worry in my heart.

"Where were you both the most intimate?" Donna asked. "I mean, which area were you not influenced by the curse or by spells?"

Donna had noticed the Kels, and had mentioned them shortly after she arrived. She was concerned they were somehow involved. The people of Chemeketa were deeply respectful of the Kels, but just as fearful of their power. Mostly, I believed, because the Kels were so secretive, and few had the ability to enter their sacred spaces within the old-growth forest.

I assured her the Kels were protective. The spell that had been cast on me was a guardian spell. It was meant to protect me. Unfortunately, it didn't appear to protect Crea.

I thought of the waterfall and the cave behind it. I didn't remember either of us being driven during our time there. It was gentler, loving, and even exploratory. "The caves," I said. "I think that has to be the caves."

Everyone here but Jennie knew what I was talking about. It wasn't like the caves were that well known, or that many people in Chemeketa knew how to find them, but Donna was on the council and belonged to the Earth Guild. The leaders of all four Guilds used that area for a Summer Solstice ceremony because it encompassed all four elements at once—water from the waterfall, air also because of the waterfall, earth because of the cave, and volcanic fire having created it.

"Then that's where we should cast the spell," Indigo said. "And hope that you and he are bonded enough for you to reach him."

"I'm his family. Would it help if I did something, or is there a spell for me to connect with him?" It was clear we'd all forgotten Jennie was there.

As a non-native to Chemeketa or the ways of our people, we wouldn't have usually incorporated her into our discussion regarding spells or the ways of the spirit realms, but because this was a crisis, we'd reacted without thinking about her.

Indigo went over and placed her hand on Jennie's shoulder. "This is stuff I know you don't understand, and it's all new to you. We have no expectations that you will participate. Regarding your question, we don't really know. It's possible, but because the curse is specifically about his romantic relationships with other men, Eli's connection, if it's strong enough, is our best chance of reaching him."

Jennie nodded. "I know I'm not from here, but I do know a little... um, my friend Scarlett told me about how this area was mostly settled by pagans, and many still practiced. I'm... well, I'm willing to learn if it helps Uncle Crea."

Indigo smiled at the young woman. "You have a strong power inside you. I've noticed it from the beginning. We can show you if you want, but for today, it may be enough just for you to be in the circle. I'll be your guide, though. If you have questions or get concerned during the spellcasting, you can let me know, and I'll help you through it."

Jennie nodded, but I could tell she was still nervous.

I led the way down the mountain toward the caves, but only got half a mile in before Ed and Lydia met us on the trail. "You'll need all the support you can get," Ed said.

I didn't ask how they knew, but I assumed the Kel spirits had alerted them to the crisis. I couldn't see them, but I knew there were more Kels there in the woods behind them. I embraced Ed and Lydia, then thanked them. "We need all the help we can get."

I led the group through the hidden rock path to access the cave.

Ed and Lydia stayed outside, and I could feel their presence surrounding the cave. That was something new for me, and I realized it had everything to do with the Kel guardian spirit that was now a part of me.

I led them to the spot where Crea and I had made love. It felt like I was exposing myself to the group having them here after we'd been so intimate, but if it helped bring Crea back, then I'd gladly do whatever was necessary.

Lee built a fire on the spot with logs and twigs the group had collected from the nearby forest. Indigo sat down on a fallen log next to Jennie, and pulled out a pouch to show her. "I'm a hedge witch like your friend Scarlett. We often use herbs, spices, and other things to accentuate our spells."

Jennie looked at the bag and asked, "What's in it?"

Indigo chuckled. "Oh, lots of lovely things. There's cinnamon to bring love and power, lavender for inner peace, lemon rind to bring a lover back, and rose to bind the spell. I also added some cayenne powder to force the spell to manifest itself quickly. We don't usually do that, but this is a bit of an emergency."

Jennie nodded, but I could tell she was still confused. Indigo soothed her by putting an arm around her shoulder and side hugged her. "You'll learn all you want to in time. For now, just know we are doing what we can for Crea."

This seemed to mollify her because she smiled nervously and nodded.

Donna poured salt around the flames, creating a circle of protection. Indigo took Jennie's hand, and explained, "We use salt to purify and cleanse an area as well as to protect us. Nobody wants anything nasty slipping in while casting a spell."

I felt the circle close as Donna finished with the salt. Combined with the circle the Kels had created outside the cave, it felt impenetrable.

Indigo and Donna stood opposite each other, and directed the rest of us to join hands. The moment we did, I felt more than heard the Kels start chanting outside.

Indigo reached into her pocket and drew out a leather bag. *"Earth and water, fire, and air, four elements combined as we speak this prayer!"* She poured the contents of the bag onto the fire, which leaped greedily to consume it.

Donna lifted her arms toward the flame, still holding my and Jennie's hands. *"Family, friends, and a lover have gathered. We call out to Brother Crea, may he know how much he matters."*

Lee began to hum low and deep, something I'd only heard him do a couple times.

As soon as the humming started, Jennie's eyes filmed over, and she began to hum in harmony with Lee. The effect was both eerie and comforting.

I reached into my pocket, letting my instincts guide me, and took the wood and emerald amulet into my hand as I began to chant, *"I sacrifice this gift from thee, who found me injured by a wayward tree. We feel your need and stand within these stones, so you will have us and not be alone."*

I placed the amulet in the fire, and immediately a green flame leaped from it. When I looked around, all four of our friends were humming, eyes glazed.

I fell to my knees then, and tears fell from my eyes as I watched the amulet burn. "Come back to me, Crea, give us a chance, please don't give up yet."

I didn't know how long we stayed like that, but when I looked up again, the fire was out. Donna, Lee, Indigo, and Jennie were standing, eyes closed, no longer humming their eerie melody. Inside the fire pit where the amulet was laid was a perfect emerald heart, polished as if by a craftsman. I reached out and took the heart in my hand. The moment my hand encased it, the spell was broken, and my four companions woke up.

I held the heart in my palm, and all four of them came to see it. "It's beautiful," Jennie said. "Amazing."

Indigo put her arm around Jennie's shoulders. We could all imagine how overwhelming this was to someone who'd never been involved in a circle before.

I could no longer feel the Kels outside the cave.

I put the beautiful heart in my pocket and led the group out of the cave, back to the cabin. We were all exhausted, as was often the case when spellcasting.

Donna took her leave, and the rest of us went to our respective rooms to rest.

I said a quiet prayer that the spell had reached Crea, that he'd heard us and would be strong enough to fight off whatever he was facing.

CHAPTER TWENTY-TWO

CREA

THE DEMON WOLF CHASED me all the way back to San Francisco. The drive took the rest of the night and into the next day, and had it not been for my fear for Chemeketa and Eli especially, I think I would've fallen asleep.

When I got home, I closed all the windows and locked the doors. I found candles and lit them like I'd seen my grandmother do when she wanted to ward off evil spirits, but nothing shed the feeling of being watched.

I was afraid to sleep. Now that I didn't have the ring, I felt vulnerable. As if, at any moment, the monsters could burst into my home and devour me.

I sat in the most uncomfortable piece of furniture I had, sure that sitting there would keep me awake. Nothing helped, though, and I was asleep within a few moments of sitting down.

I was back in the forests around Chemeketa, but they weren't the same. These were eerie, full of malice, and the place felt sickly, cold, and dark. I heard the wolf before I saw it and began to run. It chased me, teasing me.

I knew I was going to die there, and to be honest, I was okay with that. I almost wanted it. I would be done with it once and for all. The only thing that kept me from facing the wolf, giving into my father's curse, was the thought that if I did, it would have the strength to destroy my brothers. That it would go after them next.

I ran for what felt like hours, hiding in thickets of blackberry bushes that scratched me and drew blood. The scratches were different, though. They burned and festered with poison, making me feel less and less hopeful.

Eventually, I felt as if I could no longer run. I fell down a deep ravine and felt my ankle snap. The wolf came, and I saw its eyes, the wicked lust for my blood. I closed my eyes as it reared back on his hind legs to leap, when I heard a melody surrounding me. I opened my eyes to see a light coming from my hand, and when I opened it, the ring was there. I slipped it onto my middle finger.

I turned to the wolf, wondering why it had yet to attack, and noticed it stood away from the light the ring was emitting. I got to my knees, ignoring the pain in my ankle, and pushed the ring toward the animal, who leaped back to avoid it.

The wolf snarled at me and ran off into the trees. I could tell it was still close by, still watching me, but with the ring back, I at least had some protection. I tightened my fist, fairly certain that even though it was loose, it wasn't likely to fall off.

I got up then and began hobbling, using the trees to support me and keep as much weight off my ankle as possible. I moved toward the sound of water in the distance. "Maybe this was the way to the cave," I wondered aloud, or at least hoped. The cave could give me shelter and keep the wolf at bay.

CHAPTER TWENTY-THREE

ELI

I FINALLY LAY DOWN on my bed, closing my eyes, and the moment I did, I was face to face with Crea's grandmother.

"You have to go to him," she said. "He needs you. I've given him the ring back, he lost it in the forest, but it won't keep him safe forever. He needs to trust in himself, in his strength of heart, to survive. He needs you to show him his heart is strong."

The woman was frantic. I could tell we were in the forest, but it felt different, not the same as the forest that surrounded the cabin.

I rushed down the path the old woman pointed toward, a path I'd never seen before, but I knew it was the way to Crea. "Here"—she handed me a long staff—"use this," she said, before disappearing.

I heard and felt the negative energy around me. It was completely opposite to the energy that surrounded us when we cast the spell in the waterfall cave.

I knew Crea was there, and I knew he was in danger.

I saw the wolf running ahead of me, but the heart that had been formed during the spell was warm in my pocket. Its power was radiating through me. I no longer feared the wolf, at least not for myself. I feared what it could do to Crea.

I came around a corner and saw the path ended at a cliff. Water from a river flowed off the cliff, and I could hear the waterfall roaring as it fell.

I saw the wolf standing in my path before I noticed Crea standing on the edge of the abyss.

"Crea," I yelled, but the waterfall was so loud he couldn't hear me. I veered off the path, and circled the wolf, who watched me warily, continuously putting itself between Crea and me.

I managed to get close enough to Crea to notice his ring was glowing. It seemed to be keeping the wolf away because I was able to get close enough that he could understand me.

"Crea," I called again.

He looked at me then, surprise alighting his face. As quickly as the expression came, though, it disappeared.

"Leave me alone," he called out at me, or maybe he was talking to the wolf. We were both the same distance from him.

"Listen, Crea, I'm here, I've got your back. I just need you to come to me, okay?"

The wolf shifted forms and took on the shape of a man. "You can't trust him, he can't love you, none of them can. You should jump. End it now. Save yourself and him at the same time."

"Crea, don't listen to him. It's the curse talking. You can stop this, you can stop him, but you have to trust yourself."

The demon man began walking toward Crea, and I knew he would reach him before I did. I looked down at the staff his grandmother had given me, and for the first time, saw the end had a slit cut into it. The heart in my pocket grew warm, and I reached in, pulled it out, and fitted it into the slit. When I looked at it again, I realized this wasn't a staff, it was a spear.

"Crea," I yelled, "catch!"

I tossed the spear to him, and he caught it just as the man turned back into a wolf and pounced.

Instinct took over, and Crea crouched, holding the spear in such a way the wolf impaled himself on it, headfirst.

A bright light emanated from the end of the spear and from the ring on Crea's hand, both at the same time. The howl was intense, and I was afraid the impact was enough to throw Crea over the edge of the waterfall.

I'd rushed forward when the wolf or man or demon... whatever it was, had leaped, so within seconds I finally reached him. The impaled creature was disappearing as I caught Crea in my arms.

He wept as I held him. I must have had my eyes closed because when I opened them, we were no longer in the creepy forest on the edge of an abyss. We were back in the cave... our cave.

"Are you okay?" I asked as I pulled him back.

He nodded. "I'm sorry. I was stupid to leave, I was..."

"Shh, no need to explain. I know why you left, but you don't have to run away again, I'm here. I plan to be here as long as you want or need me, okay?"

He nodded and we embraced.

"Eli?" he said when we pulled apart.

"Hmm," I said.

"I think I have feelings for you. I think that's what saved me, saved us."

I nodded and smiled. "I think I have feelings for you too, and I agree, I think that's what saved us."

Another tear slipped down his cheek, and I pulled him to me, kissing him and tasting the salty tear on his lips.

When we pulled apart, I looked down and saw his hand. "What's that?" I asked. "Are you hurt?"

He looked at where the ring had been just moments before, and on the back of his hand, visible though bloodied, was a heart-shaped tattoo that glowed bright green.

"You too," he said, and I looked down and saw the same distinctive tattoo on my hand, only opposite to Crea's.

"That's something," I said, and when I looked back at Crea, he was smiling.

"It's something good, right?" he asked.

"Yeah, it's something real good. I think it means we're bonded."

"Well, yeah, but you still owe me a date."

I laughed out loud and pulled him back into my arms. "I promise, we'll go on lots of them."

"I'm going to take the job in Chemeketa," he said when he pulled back.

"Yeah, me too."

"Wanna rent me a room?" he asked, and laughed.

"I would love to have you be my roommate, although there's going to be a lot of construction going on for a while. Think you can handle that?" I asked.

He smiled. "Yeah, I can handle that."

He glanced around the cave. "Um, are we still dreaming?"

I looked at the waterfall, the dirt on the ground, along with the small burnt pile we'd made earlier, and said, "Um, no, I think we're actually here."

He sighed. "Well, I'm going to have to fly back to San Francisco to get my car."

I laughed. "I think we'll figure all that out later."

We stood up, and he winced at the pain in his ankle. "Shit, that's real too."

I took his shoe off, and I could tell that the ankle was sprained, or worse.

"Want me to go get help?" I asked.

Fear crossed his face. "No, I definitely don't want to be left alone!"

"Okay, let's try to get you back to the cabin."

We hobbled up the path together, and it seemed like hours before we finally made it back. I pushed the door open, and the entire crew was sitting around the empty fireplace in silence. When they saw us, they all rushed forward.

"Where have you been?"

"Are you okay?"

They all spoke at once, and I put my hand up. "I'll tell you after we get Crea onto the sofa with his foot elevated. Can someone get him an icepack?" Lee helped me maneuver Crea onto the cushions while Indigo grabbed some ice from the kitchen.

"You came back," Jennie said to her uncle, relief at seeing him clear on her face.

"Well, not entirely by choice, not today anyway," he said, giving me a sweet smile despite the pain of his ankle.

"Where's your car?" she asked.

"San Francisco," he said, and her mouth dropped.

"No way. You teleported here?"

He chuckled. "Not exactly. I'm not sure what you'd call it, but I don't recommend it as a future travel option!"

Chapter Twenty-Four

Crea

I CONTACTED DONNA THE following day, and told her I was a yes for the farm manager job at the Grange House. To be honest, now that I'd accepted it, I couldn't quite understand my hesitation. Sure, I wasn't going to be part of the fast-paced San Francisco lifestyle, but that hardly mattered to me any longer. As I grew older, I spent less and less time at clubs and more time with friends, or working in the gardens I managed.

Eli had yet to commit to the forester job. They were still ironing out all the details of his commitments. Regardless of how I felt about him, or that we'd committed to continuing our relationship, I decided I wouldn't be living my life in the shadow of anyone. I could tell my part of the curse had been lifted, but that just meant we could choose a relationship, not that we would have one.

After speaking with Mr. Henry, I agreed to rent a room from him, at least for a while. He lived close to the Grange House, which would be nice as we were beginning the project.

I finished my two weeks in San Francisco and listed my home for sale. The house sold less than a week after it went on the market. My little nineteen twenties bungalow, which I'd paid an arm and a leg for when I'd moved there, sold for triple what I'd paid for it. So, even after I'd paid off what was left of the mortgage, I had a nice nest egg for the future.

The fact that I didn't really have friends that were upset by my departure also spoke volumes. When I'd left Seattle and hell, even when I'd left Chemeketa, people were sad to see me go. The only people upset by my leaving San Francisco were my clients.

Eli, Jennie, Lee, and Indigo all showed up with two trucks to help me move. The contrast between people I'd known for years, and people I'd just met but felt like family, also spoke volumes about the choice I'd made to move.

While I finished my two weeks, I drew up plans for the new garden project to have approved by my new committee, and hoped the Earth Guild would approve it sooner rather than later. My plan created a large section behind the Grange House that would have access to water from the building. This would be our community gardens. If needed, we could create over a hundred eight-by-four-foot gardens over a period of time.

I wanted to experiment with a few methods that had worked well in larger farming programs in the city. Having so many dairy farms in the area led to a wonderful opportunity to use natural compost, which I, of course, wanted to use.

I knew I was thinking too far ahead into the future. I always had grandiose ideas when planning and had to pull myself back, but it felt good to be excited about the projects ahead.

After helping me put my stuff in storage, close to Chemeketa, I moved into the room above Mr. Henry's garage. The man was so sweet, he loved to cook, and I realized if I didn't get a hell of a lot more exercise, I would end up being the size of a barn. I began jogging in the mornings, which was how I learned I'd become mist phobic. That didn't work too well living in this region. Hell, two-thirds of the year, the area was a rainforest. I usually didn't go much further than the end of the driveway when the days were rainy, but I figured over time, I'd learn not to be quite so afraid.

Fall came quickly, and with it, Eli's decision to become a forester. He didn't need the salary because, as he told the council, "I've made more than I'll ever use even if I live three lifetimes." So, it was decided that an understudy would be hired from the community to work with him and Lee, ensuring that even when the two men weren't available, someone would be looking out for the forest.

Eli would take over the log cabin on top of the mountain. He purchased the sawmill in town and moved his workshop there, which, of course, brought a lot of attention from residents. Jennie was much more people-friendly than Eli, so the shop was open to visitors only when Eli was in the forest.

I moved in with him right before the Winter Solstice, after he'd completely renovated the kitchen and bathrooms. The rest of the house was in perfect shape. Other than removing a lot of shag carpeting and buffing and shining the original floors, the home was ready for habitation by the time the Solstice came around.

The front house renovation was scheduled for spring after the worst of the rains had dissipated. This part of Chemeketa got much more snow than the lower parts, because of the elevation. So, it wasn't wise to begin a project of that size until warmer weather prevailed.

We cuddled together on the new oversized sofa we'd purchased while on one of our shopping excursions to Portland, watching the yule log burn. Eli's sculpture gift he'd given me sitting pride of place on the other side of the fire pit.

I'd fallen asleep in his arms, and only woke when he shifted his weight under me. I looked up and saw him staring at the log, and said, "In the tradition of new beginnings..." He looked down at me and smiled. "I love you," I said.

He wrapped his arms tighter around me and nuzzled my hair. "I love you too, and have for a long time," he said.

"Why didn't you say something?" I asked

"'Cause I knew you weren't ready to hear it."

I snuggled back into him again. "I'm ready to hear it now. In fact, I want to hear it over and over."

He chuckled and kissed the top of my head. "I love you, my dearest Crea, and plan to love you forever."

I hummed at how wonderful those words made me feel. I looked down at my hand and saw the heart-shaped tattoo that had all but disappeared when my hand had healed was glowing emerald.

Eli showed me his, and it, too, was glowing. "Guess that's gonna show up when we express our love for each other, huh?"

Eli chuckled. "No, I'm guessing it'll show up anytime we do anything as a couple. It's a symbol of what we are together, I think."

"I like that," I said sleepily and yawned.

Eli shifted, then pulled us both up to the remodeled master bedroom. "Let's go celebrate the new year and let me show you just how much I love you," he said.

"Will it be different from how you showed me earlier today?" I asked.

"Sure, 'cause I don't have to bite back the words now. I can scream 'I love you' along with your name this time."

I laughed. I'd been biting back the same words, so I knew exactly what he meant.

CHAPTER TWENTY-FIVE

MEANWHILE...

THE DARK SMOG-LIKE MIST curled around the deject-ed man as he lay in the hospital bed. The stroke had rendered him mostly helpless. Since he'd cast the curse that had shattered his family, he'd had to fight the darkness that constantly threatened to engulf him.

Unfortunately, the stroke had left him unable to fight any longer. The result was that the dark had begun to infiltrate his mind.

"They won this one"—the mist whispered in his ear as its inky tendrils wound around him—"but you have no reason to worry. No, they will not beat us again." Its laughter was sinister. "We will win, because there is nothing that feeds the dark more than a parent who betrays his children."

Join Blake's email list to get advance notice of new books and receive his occasional newsletter:

www.blakeallwood.com

MM Romance
By Blake Allwood

Transitions Series
Aiden Inspired
Suzie Empowered (MF Romance)
Bobby Transformed

Chance Series
Love By Chance
Another Chance With Love
Taking A Chance For Love

Romantic Series
Romantic Renovations (1)
Romantic Rescue (2)
Romantic Recon (3)

Melody Series
Melody of the Heart
Melody of the Snow

Road to Rocktoberfest Anthology
Changing His Tune - 2022

Coming Home Series (2023)
A Long Way Home
Family Home
Down Home
…and many more

Novellas
Tenacious
Moon's Place

Romantic Fantasy
By Adam J. Ridley

Big Bend Series
Love's Legacy (1)
Love's Heirloom (2)
Love's Bequest (3)

The Witch Brothers Series
Emerald Earth
Diamond Air
Ruby Fire
Sapphire Water

Blake Allwood was born in west Tennessee, then moved to Kansas City MO after earning a degree in Early Childhood Education from Graceland College in Lamoni, Iowa. He met his husband Shaun in 1995 and they officially married in 2015, once gay marriage was legalized; although they still consider Valentines Day 1995 as their true "anniversary date". Twenty-two years later (2017), after fostering 12 children together, he and his husband sold their home, purchased an RV and began traveling the country with their two dogs.

Typically, Blake can be found relaxing in the RV or by the fire with his laptop and their Jack Russell Terrier, Buddy, curled up between his legs demanding attention. Denver, their Siberian Husky mix is often asleep at his feet or playing tug of war with Blake's husband.

Most of Blake's stories are inspired by the places they have visited in their ongoing travels. His first book, ***Aiden Inspired***, was released in 2019 and he has now written over 20 books. In 2023 he is releasing the ***Coming Home*** series which is comprised of ten-plus sweet contemporary romance novels that are based on a fictional town in his home state of Tennessee.

Blake also writes under the pen name of Adam J. Ridley for his urban fantasy fans looking for stories revolving around gay characters. His first series is The Witch Brothers Saga, starting with **Emerald Earth**.